THE ZOO

USSR, 1953: Yuri Zipit lives in the staff block of The Kapital Zoo with his Papa, a specialist in animal neurology. Although Yuri is only twelve and a half, he knows plenty too. He knows an impressive array of new and complicated words — and the importance of guarding his tongue. He knows his pride in his father — and that it's a crime to love your family more than you love Socialism. But he doesn't know what's just around the corner for him and his Papa, when they are dragged off in the middle of the night to visit some very important people . . .

CHRISTOPHER WILSON

THE ZOO

Complete and Unabridged

ULVERSCROFT
Leicester

First published in Great Britain in 2017 by
Faber & Faber Ltd
London

First Large Print Edition
published 2017
by arrangement with
Faber & Faber Ltd
London

A catalogue record for this book is available
from the British Library.

ISBN 978–1–4448–3483–3

Published by
F. A. Thorpe (Publishing)
Anstey, Leicestershire

Set by Words & Graphics Ltd.
Anstey, Leicestershire
Printed and bound in Great Britain by
T. J. International Ltd., Padstow, Cornwall

For Fiona, Sophie and Ben

Hope is the thing with feathers
That perches in the soul
And sings the tune without the words
And never stops at all

EMILY DICKINSON

With many thanks to Jonny Geller, Louisa Joyner and Kate Cooper.

1

Over My Head in History

The Kapital, 1954

My class teacher, Comrade Professor Mikhail Mikhailov, says in Amerika they have one hundred and seventy-three flavours of ice-cream and three hundred and seventy-six different models of motor car. While, here, in the Union of Socialist Republics we have five types of motor car. All black. And ice-cream is ice-cream flavoured, or chocolate.

All the same, in Kapitalist USA they despise other peoples, especially the black man, and their movies are always about being richer than your neighbours, kissing showgirls and killing foreigners. Even the comedies. While here in the Motherland, we have Comradeship, Justice-For-All, Freedom-in-One-Country, and the other fine thing. The one that begins with an 's' and ends with an 'ism'. Besides the whatsit that ends with an 'ology'. Even for the Chechens and Azer-baijanis. And sometimes Gypsies. For Jews too. So I know which is the place for money to prosper, and which is the better place for people.

★ ★ ★

Call me Yuri. Though I get called lots of names, such as *Yuri nine-fingers*, *Yuri the Confessor*, or *Yuri the Deathless*. But my full, formal title is Yuri Romanovich Zipit.

I am twelve-and-a-half years old and I live in the staff apartments, in The Kapital Zoo, facing the sea-lions' pool, behind the bisons' paddock, next to the elephant enclosure, and I like to play the piano but I am no Sergei Rachmaninov because my right arm is crooked and stiff, so I mostly play one-handed pieces, such as are written for the army of one-armed veterans, who sacrificed a limb for the Motherland, fighting in the Great Patriotic War.

I am in the Junior Pioneers Under-Thirteens Football Team, but I am no Lev Yashin. Mostly, I play fourth reserve, because of my limping legs, which stop me running, so I get to carry the water bottles. I am good at biology but I am no Ivan Pavlov.

I am damaged. But only in my body. And mind. Not in my spirit, which is strong and unbroken.

When I was six-and-one-quarter years old I

cross paths with worst luck. A milk truck smacks me from behind while I am crossing Yermilova Street. It sends me tumbling somersaults through the air before bringing me down to earth, head first on the cobbles. Then a tram comes along, and runs me over, behind my back.

Things like this leave a lasting impression.

But Papa always encourages me to make the most of my misfortunities. He says 'Every wall has a door' and 'What doesn't kill you makes you stronger.'

And whenever you complain to him, about anything — like injustice, weevils in porridge, getting punched on the nose at school, a broken leg, or losing fifty kopecks — he says, 'Well, count yourself lucky. There are worse things in life.'

As it turns out, he's three-quarters right. In time, all the bits of my head joined back together. Open wounds healed. Bones set. My legs mended, most parts. But there are some breaks in my brain, mostly in my thinking-departments, and without any clear memories of whatever came before.

I have some holes in my memory still. Sometimes I choose the wrong words. Or I can't find the right one, and lay my hands on the real meanings. Facts fly out of my windows. My feelings can curdle like sour

3

milk. Sense gets knotted. Then it's hard to untangle my knowledge. I don't concentrate easily.

Other times I cry for no good reason. Except I am throbbing with sadness. Sometimes, I go dizzy and fall over. Then there are flashes of brilliant light — orange, gold and purple — and odd, nasty smells — like singed hair, pickled herring, carbolic, armpits and rotting lemons. Then I lose consciousness. They tell me I thrash about on the ground. And dribble frothy saliva. And ooze yellow snot through my nose. This is when I am having a fit. Afterwards I can't remember any of it. But I have new bruises, which is a good thing, because it is my body's way to remember for me what my brain has forgotten. Maybe I need to change my trousers, as a matter of urgency.

So I am sometimes slow and forgetful. Except in recreations and games — like battleships, hang-the-Fascist, chess and draughts — where I excel, because then everything I need to know lies seen, and open, there in front of me. So I can just play the game, without having to remember what happened on Thursday morning, how many sides on a dodecahedron, how to spell coccyx, or the Kapital of Uzbekistan.

So, overall, Papa tells me, the fool in me is

finely balanced by my cleverness. And he calls me a *pochemuchka*. A child who asks too many questions. Without a brake on his mouth.

Plus I have another problem. It's the unfortunate look of my face.

People keep staring at it. My face. And then start seeing things. That just aren't there.

They gaze at me. They stare like an animal caught in headlights. Then they break into a smile. Then I smile back. Before you know it we're talking. And, by then, we're lost. It's too late.

Papa says folk can't help it. They see sympathy in my features. They find kindness in my eyes. They read friendliness in the split of my smiling mouth.

Guess what? They think I care about them. Even though they're total, absolute, hundred-per-cent strangers. They think they know me. From somewhere. But they can't remember where.

Papa says my appearance is a fraud and a bare-faced liar. He says that — although I am a good child in many ways, and kind enough — I am not half as good as my face pretends.

Papa says my face is one of those quirks of inheritance, when two ordinary parents can mix to produce something extreme and striking. You see it too with moths, orchids and axolotls.

He says my face is my very best, prize-winning quality. He says my smile is easy and wide. My features are neat and regular. My gaze is direct but gentle. It lends me a sweet and tender face. The very kindest face you'd hope to find. A face that seems to love whoever it looks upon.

Papa says it is a face that could have been painted by the Italian artist Sandro Botticelli, to show an angel on his best behaviour, sucking up to God.

It gives me grief, my sympathetic, wide-open, smiling face. Papa says I have a true genius for needless and reckless involvement in the private affairs of other people.

Also he observes I am foolhardy.

Beyond idiocy.

And that I talk without first thinking.

'Shhh . . . ' he always says. 'Idiot child.'

He says that when my head hit the cobbles of Yermilova Street, every fragment of fear got shaken out. Now my Frontal Lobes are empty, he says. My common sense went next. Closely followed by my tact, and then my inhibitions.

Of course, there's a name for my condition. I suffer from *impulsivity* brought on by *cerebral trauma*. Which is a way of saying I talk a lot, and move a lot, and ask a lot of questions, and make up my mind quickly, and do things on the spur of the moment, and find new solutions to things, and say rude things without thinking, and interrupt people to tell them when they've got things wrong, and blurt things out, and change my mind, and make strange animal noises, and show lots of feelings, and get impatient, and act unexpectedly. All of which makes me like other people. But more so.

Because I make friends easily. With people and with animals. I enjoy talking. To anyone, more or less. And meeting new animals. Especially new species who I have never had the fortune to converse with before.

I like to help. Even strangers. After all, we are all chums and Comrades, put in this life to help each other, and rub along together.

In particular, I provoke whatever you call it when *people-tell-you-too-much-about-themselves, even-though-it-is-secret-and-shameful, concerning-things-that-you-never wanted-or-expected-to-hear, and-are-probably-best-kept-secret, unspoken, for-all-concerned.*

Like a *confidence,* but even worse.

A magnet attracts iron-filings. I attract confessions. Strongly. From all directions.

I only have to show my face in public and total strangers form an orderly line, like a kvass queue, to spill their secrets into my ears.

Soon, their honesties turn ugly.

'I am a useless drunk.' One says.

Or 'I cheat on my wife, on Thursday afternoons, with Ludmilla, with the squint, from the paint depot, whose breasts smell of turpentine. By chance, she's my brother's wife . . . '

Or 'I killed Igor Villodin. I hacked off his head with a spade . . . '

Or 'It was me who stole the postage stamps from the safe in the bicycle-factory office . . . '

Often they flush with shame. Sometimes they start sobbing. They pull terrible gurning faces or gesture wildly with their hands.

Then I have to say, 'I am sorry . . . but you are confusing me with my face. It's much kinder than me, but it's not to be trusted . . . Of course, I like you . . . But I cannot take on everyone's problems. Not all the time. I have a young life of my own to live.'

'Anyway,' I say, 'don't worry. Things are never so bad as you imagine. Everything considered . . . What is done is done. What doesn't kill you makes you stronger. Every wall has a door. Make the most of your misfortunities. They make you what you are in life, and different from all other people. This is the only life you get. You must pick yourself up and move on.'

Aunt Natascha says everyone wants to confess in life, like Raskolnikov in *Crime and*

Punishment, because they need to be understood and find forgiveness somewhere.

And since Lenin did away with God, Praise the Lord, may he rest in peace, they must look elsewhere, and closer to home.

So, they pick on me.

And I encourage confidences, she says, because I am friendly, and my face tells them I possess a gentle kindness that can forgive them anything.

It's then that she tells me that she despises Uncle Ivan, because he is a pervert, of the sickest sort, always trying to kiss her, and putting his hand up her skirt, to touch her thingammy, demanding rumpty-tumpty, day and night, any room in the house, and so she wishes he were dead.

But if you ask me to choose my favourite meal, I would say Polish pork sausage with buttered cabbage and potatoes fried in goose fat. I admit it. Topped with braised onions on the side. I should be so lucky. With wild mushrooms in sour cream dressing. And for dessert I would have blueberries with ice-cream. In my dreams.

By choice, I would drink birch juice or cherry nectar each and every mealtime. My favourite colour is scarlet. Because it is the colour of excitement, Saturday, Revolution, our flag, and Dynamo Kapital football shirts.

My favourite player is The Black Spider, goalkeeper Lev Ivanovich Yashin. My name day is November 18th. My special hobby is studying wild animals. I am a member of the Young Biologist Club of The Kapital Zoo. My favourite zoo animal is the Brown Bear (*Ursus arctos*) and my favourite rodent is Severtzov's Birch Mouse (*Sicista severtzovi*).

★ ★ ★

My Papa is Doctor Roman Alexandrovich Zipit — Professor of Veterinary Science — who specialises in Cordate Neurology, which is the study of whatever goes wrong inside the brains of animals, so long as they have a backbone, especially in The Kapital Zoo.

You've maybe heard of him. Most likely you'll have seen his photograph in *The Progressive Journal of Socialist Neurology*. He is well regarded around The Kapital, in the mental community and sick-animal circles. His writings are well known to almost everyone who closely attends the brains of elephants.

And because he is a world famous, respected veterinarian he gets to treat world famous animals including Count Igor, the Juggling Tiger in the State Circus, Golden Glinka the racehorse and Comrade Composer Shostakovich's Fox Terrier Tomka.

But I never brag about being the son of a famous man, because bragging comes before a fall. And Papa's nothing special. Not to look at. Not from the outside. Not so you'd notice. So you would have to unscrew his head and shine a torch into the depths of his fantastic, huge brain to see what is peculiar about him. And if you met him on the street you wouldn't think twice, except to admire his overcoat with the astrakhan collar. Besides he's bald with a limp and a stoop, and carries a musty scent along with a tarry taint of pipe tobacco.

★　★　★

The things I am going to tell you are all true. Absolutely, completely, totally true.

Almost.

Except for the small things I change. Because I have to.

But only events, times, names and places.

Because these are very complicated and most confidential affairs, and shady events, leading to dark happenings.

These are secrets hiding away in history.

I am trusting to your silence. Also, I have to protect you.

For your own safety.

So, shhh.

It would harm you to speak of any of this. Because you shouldn't know it. Not any of it. So best keep quiet as a mouse. And blind as a mole.

Even now, I don't understand everything. To grasp it all you would need to speak Georgian like a native, tell dirty jokes like a Mingrelian secret policeman, have a reindeer-horn pocket knife, with one of those special can-opener attachments, be able to drink two bottles of pepper vodka and still stay sober, be a consultant in Neurology, and a senior member of the Politburo, with a doctorate in assassinations.

Things are hidden within other things, like a nest of wooden dolls. There's murder, medicine, theatre, cookery, juggling, skulduggery, impersonation, elephants, fate, within a whodunit, inside a mystery, wrapped in a tissue of lies, stuffed in a cardboard box, locked up in the under-stairs cupboard.

★　★　★

The events I write about began in 1953, one year ago, in Karasovo, near The Kapital, when Papa and I get dragged off in the middle of the night to visit some very important people.

More than important, I'd say.

No lie.

Particularly Scarface Joe, Felix the Juggler, Alexei the Actor, Lev, Georgy, Nikita, Nicolai, Matryona the Maid, and shit-face-Erik.

But don't be fooled too easily. These are not their actual, factual names. It is dangerous to speak their full, real names. Ditto, real places. And other stuff.

Trust me.

There are several titles and personages I cannot even mention — like the Gardener of Human Happiness, Engineer of Human Souls, First Secretary, Deputy Prime Minister, Duty Officer, Marshal of the Slavic Union, Pavel the Gatekeeper, and whatsisname.

But spending time with the un-nameable, top-rank people you quickly get sucked deep into shit, in the sewer of politics. Forgive my Bulgarian. Before you know it, you are sunk up to your neck in trouble. Then you are over your head in history.

So let me share the advice Papa gives me —

Don't slouch. Don't smile at strangers. People misunderstand. These are grave times. Be warned. Blow your nose, you're dribbling. Pay close attention. Stop gibbering like a demented gibbon. Mind your manners. Stay on your guard. Try not to scuff your shoes when you walk. Brush your teeth, morning and evening. Get an early night when you can. Keep your head down. Change your underpants. Don't confide in strangers. Shut the door, for pity's sake. Keep your lips sealed. If people ask you awkward questions, act simple-minded. Go to the lavatory when you can. You don't know when the chance will come again. Don't prattle on like a total idiot. Above all, don't mention politics, or voice opinions off the top of your head.

Papa says the song of our time is silence, and the moral is 'Shhh.'

It's best not even to state the obvious, or hint at what everyone knows.

We are living in an age that hugs silence and befriends the mute.

Our National Anthem has become a breathless hush.

He says, if you have to open your mouth, you should make sure that whatever you say is as bald and plain as a boiled noodle, and has been first approved by a Central Committee, published in *The Daily Truth*, or incorporated into a Five Year Plan. All praise to Comrade Iron-Man, Man of Steel, Kind

Uncle, and Father of Our Nation.

Above all, you mustn't make jokes.

Especially not this one —

Question: What has a thousand legs and eats potatoes?
Answer: A Kapital meat queue.

Because that was the very pleasantry that gets Gennady Sharikov sent to the work camps for eleven years. So it's not worth telling it. Not in the long run. Just to pass the time with a stranger on a tram, who then smirks, then arrests you. Because you never know who you're talking to. It may be a plain-clothes Colonel in the People's Commissariat for Internal Affairs. And even walls have ears. Besides hunger is never funny. And it is malicious to laugh at other people's misfortunes and you-know-whats.

All that happened was very *dialectical*, which is not a foreigner's way of talking but actually a meeting of opposing forces, like two stags butting heads for one doe. So something has to give. And things can never be the same again. Papa says that is how history works, particularly Slav history, where things can just go from bad to worse, and from worse to awful, in the blink of an eye, and it's hard to get a good night's sleep, and enough to eat, and snow-proof felt boots, although the excitement, cold feet and hunger can provoke great Socialist music and heroic literature, and Social Realist painting, by way of compensations. All praise to the Party. All homage to Comrade Iron-Man.

★   ★   ★

As it happens, I love finding new words like *dialectical, epicentral, duodenum, catawampus, egregious, skulduggery, infinitesimal*, and then working them like crazy, maybe for a whole week or so, until they've lost all their shine and gone all *lackadaisical* and *lacklustre*.

But, trust me, everything that follows is as true, inedible and indelible as the scarlet birthmark on my right buttock, which Papa says looks the spit of a young Comrade Lenin in profile, facing leftwards.

2

Herman the German

I am born in 1940, with dark clouds gathering, nine months before Herman the German invades the Motherland. Even so, Papa says we mustn't hate all Fritzies, but only the Nazi scum, the Brigand Interventionist you-know-whos, the Kapitalist Hegemonist thingammies, the War-Mongers, Fascists and Imperialists, and not the decent Common Cabbage, Rubber-Neck and Potato-Head, our proletarian Hun brothers.

He says we mustn't forget there have been many good Germans, and even some great ones, who have sprinkled themselves throughout history — poets, scientists and artists, and ordinary people too — who never, not once, invaded the Socialist Union, scorched our crops, bombed our cities, plundered our homes, raped our women, slaughtered our people.

Papa can rattle off the names of heaps of good Germans, off the top of his head, just like that, exhausting the fingers of both hands — with folk like Mozart, Martin Luther, Karl Marx, Goethe, Engels, Beethoven, Kant, and

17

you-know-who — except you can't help noticing that they're mostly dead.

We live in the staff block of The Kapital Zoo. It is a two-floor building with carved shutters, a fancy gable, and a long balcony, backing onto the entrance gates, overlooking the lake. There are six apartments. Three on each whatsisname.

This way there are always the keepers, attendants and guards to take care of the animals, day and night. Because during the Great Patriotic War, we all made our contribution, animals included, and the zoo stayed open, even during the heaviest bombing. And animals often got hurt, from falling masonry or shrapnel, so Papa was on call at all times, as Chief Vet.

But sometimes there was nothing to be done but take a pistol to put an injured beast out of its misery. And then there was just a bleeding carcass, on its back with its still, splayed legs in the air. But it's a crime to waste good food in a time of famine. So we would share the meat out. The staff got some. So did the large carnivores, like the big cats. So we enjoyed some rare delicacies denied to the rest of The Kapital like Salamander Suvlaki, cabbage-stuffed Lemur, Roast Peccary with wild horseradish, and Loin of Lion, which were not traditional, Slavic dishes, but completely new to Socialist Cookery, though the meat often turned out stringy and chewy, and rarely tasted as delicious as they sounded, although most often better than stale rye bread and cold millet stew.

Papa says that the bravest, boldest beasts, like the lions and bears, never minded much about the bombing, but the ostriches, racoons, bison and deer were scared close to death. And the monkeys could never abide the blackouts, and would howl and shriek pitifully, being terrified of the gloom, because they were clever enough to fill the dark with their own imaginings.

And in 1944 the Germans bombed the power-house and blew up the generator, so the staff, and members of the Young Biologist Club, had to take the most delicate and warmth-loving animals home with them, and sometimes sleep with them in bed, which was why I came to share a cot with Petra the tiger cub and Fyodor the orphan otter, several tropical reptiles and a baby goat who was so agile he could leap from the mantelpiece to perch on the picture rail.

And I can truly say that none of them were clean or house-trained. So I often woke feeling damp in the dark. And it wasn't me that wet the bed. And, underfoot, the floorboards were often squidgy and slidy.

Once, when Fritzi drops incendiaries, a bomb lands in the enclosure of Shango the elephant. He starts pacing up and down hooting, in a strop, because he hates the horrible hissing sound it makes, and the smoke pumping out of it. Then he promptly decides to put it out by stamping it deep into the boggy ground.

And they printed an account in *The Daily Truth* under the headline *Comrade Elephant Fights Fires for The Motherland* as a lesson to everyone, to show that even the animals in The Kapital Zoo were helping out with the war effort, which was why Shango gets awarded the Order of Alexander Nevsky, for Extraordinary Contributions to the Fire Services, which is a bronze medal on a crimson ribbon with a yellow stripe, worn on the right breast, which ranks above the Order of Military Merit, even though he was a grumpy and uncomradely elephant who used his trunk to spray the visitors with shit, or hurl stones at their heads.

Now, there is just Papa and I living in our apartment. We have two bedrooms, a living room and kitchen all to ourselves because Papa is a Professor and Chief Medical Officer and because the authorities did not reassign the spare bedroom when the assistant veterinary officer Gregor Malenkov spoke out

20

of turn at a bus-stop and was called away to a camp in Kolyma.

Mama was a doctor. But she left home suddenly when I was five. This was before my accident so I have no clear pictures-in-my-mind of her. Although there are seven photos with us together. She has wavy blonde hair, fat lips and a large handsome nose. Usually she is smiling. Often she is touching me. Holding me in her arms, clutching my hand when I'm older, or hugging me. Papa is often missing, or looking grumpy at the edges. I often think how life would be different if she were still with us now.

Papa said she had gone North to do help with important medical research and would not be back for several years. And that she would not be able to write to us often. Although she still loved us both dearly.

But Andrei Maximov in my class at school told me my Mama was arrested by the People's Commissariat for Internal Affairs for being a *Socially Dangerous something-or-other* and sentenced to eight years in a work camp near Kolyma. He knows this because his uncle Modest was arrested on the same day and held in nearby cells in The Freedom and Peace Prison, although he got twelve years for doing precisely absolutely nothing at all. Zilch. Zero.

But that's Life. You don't know what to believe for the best. Because, everyone knows, for *nothing* you only get nine.

Andrei said that the police came to arrest a neighbour. But because this particular person was out, they knocked on the next door, and arrested his uncle Modest instead. Just to meet their quota.

Sometimes I wish that Papa would invite one of his three lady friends to live with us, because everyone would be happier then. And, although he knows too much about most things, his cookery lacks skill, warmth, seasoning and flavour. And his laundry lacks smoothness, dryness and whiteness. And although he is a good father, he struggles to show any feelings, and goes gruff, stiff, arm's-length and moist-eyed at the very times I need him to take some proper care of me.

Anna, Comrade Curator of Elephants, visits most, usually Tuesday and Friday evenings. She cooks a hot meal and asks me about my school-work, and who are my friends, and sews up tears in my clothes, and darns any holes in my socks. When I go to bed, she and Papa stay up and discuss Big Mammal Policy.

Then, sprawled on the sofa, they pair-off. With each other. There is mouthing, stroking, grunting, gasping and a rhythmic sound like muffled hammering. Sometimes, towards the end, Comrade Anna makes a long drawn-out sound, like a honking sea-lion, pleasured by an unexpected herring, which startles the nearby animals into silence for a moment. And the night pauses to listen, still and silent.

★   ★   ★

As long as I can remember, Papa has left two packed suitcases parked in the corridor. One for him and one for me. But they stand splayed at right angles, some metres apart. And from this, I understood, when they were needed, we would not be travelling together.

And he told me if he ever had to leave suddenly for any reason, I was to take my suitcase and leave immediately and separately for Aunt Natascha's apartment on Galinko Street. And talk only to her and no one else.

He said there were clothes, soap, toothbrush, bits and pieces and money. And some other family and personal things besides. He said I would understand what everything was for when the time came. But I should never open the case before then.

Papa says there are five new commandments to remember when dealing with strangers, to fit our modern times —

Don't think.

If you must think, then don't speak.

If you must think and speak, then don't write.

If you must think, speak and write, then don't sign.

If you must think, speak, write and sign, then don't be surprised.

It is half past seven in the evening. It is dark. The wolves are howling their evening chorus, calling for the waiters to bring their supper. The gibbons are screeching the latest monkey-gossip.

Papa and I are sitting at the pine table in the kitchen eating boiled macaroni, sprinkled with raw, grated onion.

If only all onions could be so scrumptious — purple veined, sweet, sharp and sour. Your eyes water just gazing down on them.

There is banging at the door of our apartment, hard enough to splinter the timber from its hinges. I scamper to open the door to our impatient visitors.

There are two men in the doorway, lit brightly by the bare yellow bulb on the landing. One is pale, lean and ugly. The other is pink, fat, sweaty and ugly, in a leather trench-coat, panting from climbing the stairs.

'We are here for Comrade Doctor Professor

Roman Alexandrovich Zipit,' says the lean one.

'Who is it?' Papa demands.

'It's two secret policemen,' I call back, over my shoulder. 'For *you*. A fat one who's out-of-breath, and a skinny one with yellow teeth.'

Although, if they were truly secret, and in disguise, say, to look like drunken road-sweepers, or smelly garbage-collectors, or dusty millers, we wouldn't know. But as it is, they are show-off dressers, and favour foreign clothes, which they confiscate from visitors or steal from black-marketers, so you can always see them coming.

I hear Papa scrape his bowl away from him and rise from the table. He is slow and purposeful, treading his way to us at the door, as if he has been expecting this exact interruption.

'Yes?' Father asks reluctantly. He swallows twice on air.

'We are from the Ministry of State Security, Comrade. You are to come with us immediately.'

'I have done *nothing*,' Father protests. '*Nothing* . . . ' He trails off. A note of doubt has entered his voice, as if he's just remembered doing something, after all, maybe, a while ago.

It goes without saying. Even children know.

Everyone has done *something*, sometime. If only a bit of slight stealing, or talking out of turn, or light lying, or not owning up. Anyway, it doesn't matter much. They say State Security does not make mean, personal distinctions, but treats everyone as a suspect, and every suspect as guilty.

'We know all about you.'

'You do?' asks Papa.

'Yes,' says the lean one with steel glasses, with a thin smile of rat-yellow teeth. 'We know who you married. We know your record as a student. We know what papers you have written. We know your height, your weight, your age.'

'We know your blood-type,' says the pink, sweaty one, 'the smell of your farts, your dental records, your digestive disorder, your sexual history and your fumblings in the dark. We know what happened at the conference in Smolensk, in room 147, with the lady dermatologist . . . '

'You do?' Papa blushes crimson. He sounds defeated and deflated.

'And now, you are needed,' says Pink and Sweaty. 'You are needed urgently. To treat a patient.'

'What patient?' asks Papa.

'We are not permitted to say,' says Wire Glasses.

26

'You don't need to know,' says Leather Coat.

'I'll need equipment and medicine,' says Father. 'You'd better tell me the species, and give me some idea of the problem.'

'*Species?*' asks Thin Lips.

'What kind of animal?' asks Father. He spreads his hands helplessly. 'What do you want me to treat? Is it a reptile, a bird, a mammal?'

'This is a summons to do your duty, not a game of twenty questions.' Steel Spectacles rustles his sheet of yellow paper. 'You must leave everything and come now.' He frowns down at me. He flicks his fingers to shoo me away, the way you'd dispatch a dog to its corner.

The other one has been eyeing me up, scowling, and drawing some conclusions.

I spy the bulge in his coat pocket. Anyone can tell it's a revolver.

'Do you shoot people?' I ask. 'Much?'

He says, 'Shhh.'

'With your gun?' I explain. '*There* in your pocket.' I point it out.

He scowls.

'Is it a Nagant?' I guess. 'An M1895?'

This is an old, seven-shot, double-action pistol with a heavy trigger pull. They say it is popular with secret policemen.

'Have you shortened the barrel?' I ask.

Because, often, they do.

He tells me, 'Shhh,' then turns instead to Papa and says, 'Is this unwanted noise, this smirking moron, your son?'

'The boy doesn't mean any harm. He doesn't know any better.'

'Why is he smiling at us? As if he likes us?'

'Yes, what does he mean by it?' demands the fat one.

'Does he think we are his *friends*?' asks the thin one.

'He has traumatic brain damage,' says Papa. 'From an accident. He has fits. I cannot leave him. He can't care for himself.'

I blush at becoming an imbecile. So suddenly. And without warning. The two men look to each other, unsmiling.

'Fits?'

'He has epilepsy. But he carries my equipment,' says Father. 'He is trained to act as my aide. He may be an idiot, but he is a useful idiot. I cannot work without him.'

So that's how I get my ticket for the journey alongside Papa. And we slink out into the inky night in the spitting rain, stalked by two secret policemen, with me carrying Papa's extra-large, best-quality, all eventuali-ties, leather case of instruments, not knowing if we are called to treat a mouse, or rhinoceros, or a who-knows-what.

★　★　★

Out through the turnstiles onto the pavement we are met by two uniformed policemen who walk us, their hands resting firm on our backs, to a large black car parked at the curb.

Guess what.

No lie.

This car is only one of *those*. Yes. Truly. Only a ZIS-110, six litre, eight cylinder, over one hundred and forty horse-power. Top speed one-forty kilometres per hour. Three speed transmission, not counting reverse. Electrical windscreen wipers. Directional indicators. This car is so good that the Amerikans steal the whole design to build their Packard Super-Eight.

We are in a convoy. In front is a ZIM GAZ-12 and behind a GAZ-M20 Victory. It is a parade of top class Socialist, Slavic cars.

Soon we are motoring fast, westward through Probedy Park, headlights on full beam, full speed through any stop lights. Like we are super-important people on some secret late night assignation.

3

Up to My Neck in Politics

I sense Papa's fear from his rasping, shallow breaths, and the way he leans against me, in those thick, hide-upholstered seats, clutches my hand in his hot, damp grasp, and presses my fingers hard, thinking to hold me fast.

The car throbs throaty, then growls to accelerate. We drive for many minutes. Then the buildings of The Kapital are behind us. There is woodland either side of the unlit road. We see tall watchtowers above the line of a high timber wall, painted forest green. Then we are stopped before an iron-barred gate. Sentries peer in through the car windows, dazzling us, shining their torches onto our screwed-up, scared faces.

There is a driveway up to the two-storey structure. It is a long official-looking building but there are no signs to say if it is a hospital, barracks, school, office, or what.

In the arched doorway, two fur-hatted sentries stand scowling in gold-buttoned greatcoats, with sabres in scabbards, and leather boots shiny as mirrors. There is

30

saluting, muttering, the stamping of heels, and the signing of papers as State Security passes us over, like an awkward parcel, into the care of a fat, worried-looking, bald man in a navy suit bearing the Order of Lenin medal on his lapel. Then we are bustled through the central doorway into a large wood-panelled hall, then down a long parquet-tiled corridor.

We are hurried into a small room. The heavy wooden door clicks shut behind us. We are left alone. There is a desk and chair, a sofa, and a low table stacked with papers. Next to a small square barred window, there is a wash-basin and to its side a steel rail, draped with a crisp white towel.

I see on the desk, there is a stack of Herzegovina Flor cigarette packets, a large white china ashtray with a cherry-wood pipe, like Uncle Vlad's, a pale green glass bottle of Borjomi mineral water and a drinking glass, on a fat book called *Pharaoh* by Boleslaw Prus, next to a copy of *The Combat History of the 2nd Guards Tank Army from Kursk to Berlin: Volume 1: January 1943 — June 1944*, opened at page 103.

We do not presume to sit. Not in the apartment of a *Personage*.

'But who lives here?' I whisper.

'Shhh . . . ' Papa shrugs and holds an upright finger to his lips.

'It stinks . . . ' I say. 'Pipe tobacco, wood polish, socks and armpits.'

'Shhh.' Papa shakes his head, blinks and winces.

The door opens. The worried man returns in a blur, busy as an angry wasp.

'Hurry,' he says. 'Quick, quick.' He claps his hands. 'You must not keep the Deputy waiting. Come. Come. Hurry. Hurry.'

Then we are rushed down the corridor to another door. The worried man exits, closing the door on us.

It is all very strange. For, although we have gone fifty metres down the corridor, turned a corner, and mounted a small flight of stairs, we are back ino the room that we have just left. The very same. Same walls. Same colours. Same size. Same rug. Same enamelled lampshade. Same painting of loyal workers at the Heroic Tractor Factory. There's the same desk and chair, a sofa, and a low table stacked with papers. Next to a small square barred window, there is a wash-basin and to its side a steel rail, draped with a crisp white towel.

On the desk, there is a stack of Herzegovina Flor cigarette packets, a large white china ashtray with a cherry-wood pipe, like Uncle Vlad's, a pale green glass bottle of Borjomi mineral water and a drinking glass,

on a fat book called *Pharaoh* by Boleslaw
Prus, next to a copy of *The Combat History
of the 2nd Guards Tank Army from Kursk
to Berlin: Volume 1: January 1943 — June
1944*. I happen to notice it is opened at page
103.

Only this time we are not alone. A very
short, plump man is washing his hands at the
sink. First we admire his back, muscled like a
wrestler's, stretching the seams of his taut
jacket. When he turns to face us, drying his
hands on the towel, we see, a fat, round, pale
yellow face, with bulging eyes and rimless
pince-nez. He is bald on the scalp with short
silver hair to the sides. He wears a shiny, light
blue suit, white shirt with a crimson cravat.
There is a strong smell of cologne. The hands
are white and pudgy with shiny nails.

He looks at us with cold disappointment,
as if we were his lunch, but not the dish he'd
hoped for.

I have seen his picture somewhere. Maybe
in the news-reels, or in a newspaper. He looks
comical. Perhaps he is a well-known actor, or
famous circus clown.

There are several questions I want to ask
him. And they all come out, in a rush,
together.

'Are you famous? Are you a dwarf?' I ask.
'Or just very short? What's that you smell of?

Are you wearing women's perfume? How do your glasses stay stuck on your face?'

But he just shakes his head in pained, eye-rolling silence.

Papa kicks my ankle, which is his secret code for me to hush.

'You are Doctor Roman Alexandrovich Zipit? And this smiling, loose-tongued buffoon is your simpleton son, Yuri, who acts as your assistant?'

'Exactly, Comrade,' says Papa.

'Do you know who I am?'

Father pauses, then, soft and submissive, as if reassuring a dangerous animal, he whispers, 'I believe you may be Marshal First Deputy Bruhah, Minister of Internal Affairs of the Socialist Union.'

'Perhaps,' the stranger concedes. 'But, if I were that person, you must forget ever meeting me.'

'I must.'

'Absolutely.' Comrade Maybe-Bruhah reaches out to shake Papa's hand. 'Greetings, Comrade. We have not met. Not now, not ever.'

Papa shrugs, mute, and makes a stupid, gaping smiley face.

'And yet you must wonder why you are here . . . For no purpose whatsoever . . . To meet nobody . . . in a place that does not exist . . . in the middle of the night . . . '

Papa gulps silent like a fish in a tank.

'You are here to give medical treatment to a Comrade.'

'A human being?' asks Papa. 'A person?'

'Yes.'

'*Not an animal?*'

'Absolutely,' says might-be-Bruhah. 'All of our country's leaders are human beings, excluding a couple, who are so close you'd hardly notice the difference . . . '

'Ah, but I am a *veterinarian*,' says Papa. He sounds cheerful now, spying his escape hole. 'Alas, I cannot help. I specialise in Big Mammals. Elephants and large Ungulates. Those are my forte. I do not treat people. I am not qualified. You would need to consult a *doctor*. Of *human* medicine.'

'Doctors are not to be trusted.'

'No?'

'Many are *Cosmopolitan* . . . '

'Cosmopolitan?' asks Papa.

'Jewish. *Zionist Nationalists*. Many are Amerikan spies. There is a conspiracy to kill off our leadership. There are many arrests. You will read about it shortly in the papers.'

'I did not know . . . '

'Now this patient will only trust himself to the care of *veterinarians*.'

'Indeed?' Papa frowns.

'Because veterinarians have a sound and

complete medical training. But they lack the treachery, bourgeois tendencies and Cosmopolitan habits. They are not in a conspiracy to murder our nation's leaders.'

'Yes?' Papa sounds surprised by this account of his profession.

'You will think you recognise the patient.'

'I will?'

'Yes. At first, you will think you know him. But this is dangerous and wrong-headed. Then you will promptly realise you have never seen him before, and have no notion who he is. Because he does not resemble anyone you know. Not in the slightest.'

'Yes?' says Papa.

'You will discuss this unknown, nameless man's condition with nobody but me. Between ourselves, we will call him . . . *Comrade Elephant* . . . '

'Yes?'

'Because he is a Very Big Mammal indeed, of the type you're specialised to treat. And because he is very powerful, very wise, and very kind, except when he is angry. And because he rarely forgets, and seldom forgives.'

'Very well . . . ' Papa concedes. 'But may I first see his medical history?'

'This patient has no medical history.'

'But everyone has some medical history,'

Papa protests. 'If only by being born.'

'The Comrade is an elephant of exceedingly high standing. If he had a medical history, he would have experienced some sickness. That could be misconstrued as weakness, a failing in his vitality and power, a limit to his capacity.'

'Still, any notes would be invaluable.'

'All notes were lost or destroyed a month ago. Besides, they never existed.'

'Then, the doctors who treated him before? They will surely remember.'

'Unfortunately, those doctors barely exist. His personal physician was Marian Vovsi.'

'How do I reach him?'

'With difficulty. Since he is dead. He died of heart paralysis. He did not survive the pressing questions of my curious colleagues . . . '

'There's no one else?'

'There was a Professor Otinger.'

'The Cardiologist?'

'But now he is under arrest. Anyway, his heart gave way.'

'His colleagues?'

'Doctors Spielman, Groshtein and Kogan-Geiger are being held for criminal investigation . . . '

It sounded as if being a doctor had itself become a fatal medical condition.

Comrade Nobody-we-know leads us down the
long corridor. There is an endless patterned
carpet laid over the gleaming wood-block flooring. The air smells of scorched cabbage and
beeswax. The walls and ceiling are panelled
with darkened wood.

After we have walked perhaps fifty metres
we turn into a doorway.

Then Maybe-Marshal knocks on the heavy,
wood-panelled door and, receiving no answer,
leads us into the room.

Of course, it is the same room. The small
room we have come to expect, and have
visited twice before. Everything is as it was
— the basin, the rug, lampshade, painting of
the tractor factory, table, books, cigarette
packets, bottle of mineral water.

But the air is warmer and the smells riper
and richer. There are the scents of warm,
damp bedding, vomit, chlorine disinfectant
and stale pee.

The patient lies sprawled on his back on a
sofa. He wears a white night-shirt, risen up
above the knees, to reveal his hairless legs,
whitish with a pale blue sheen.

His eyes are closed. His breath is quick and
shallow. He releases a regular snore, mixing
rasping in-breath with rattling out-breath. His

face is grey. His lips are purpled.

If you were to ask me if I recognise him, I'd say I can't be sure. But I would remark that he bears some strong resemblances to Comrade Iron-Man.

Yes. In some ways he definitely looks like him —

The Great Father.
Kind Uncle Josef.
The Man of Iron.
The Genius.
The Inspirer.
The Gardener of Human Happiness.
Architect of Joy.
The Repository of All Hope.
Himself.
General Secretary of the Communist Party.
Saviour of Our Nation.

Except . . . *this* Sick-Man has a badly scarred face and is a scrawny, titch of a fellow with a bent left arm.

His face wears a tired, mean, wrinkled, foxy expression. While the Great Father of Our Nation, as the posters show, always wears a look of calm, kind nobility on his smooth-skinned face.

So I guess the Sick-Man might be in some way connected to share the family face — Comrade Iron-Man's older brother, cousin, or perhaps his father.

Papa has a sharp intake of breath. He stands over the man and blinks with concern. He sniffs the man's quick, shallow breath. He lays his head to the man's chest, to listen to his heart. He clutches the man's left wrist, and watches the second-hand of his wrist watch.

'*Sphygmomanometer*,' Papa demands, and I root around in his leather case for the blood-pressure cuff and mercury tube.

Papa bends and stretches and unbends the man's four limbs in turn.

'Write, Comrade Assistant . . . ' Papa hands me his notebook and his silver propelling pencil. I think he is trying to demonstrate my usefulness and a need for my presence.

'Unknown Male. Approximately seventy-five years old,' he dictates. ' . . . No distinguishing features . . . None whatsoever . . . Smallpox scarring to right and left cheek . . . Left arm stiffened. Historic damage to joints and musculature. Shorter than right arm. Webbing to left foot. Second and third toes fused . . . One and a half metres in height . . . Severe hypertension. Tachycardia. Irregular cardiac rhythm . . . Low oxygenation of toes, fingers, limbs and face . . . '

Then, to all Papa's comments I add a

scribble, of my own observation —

'Stinks like a goat.'

★ ★ ★

'So?' demands Comrade Could-be-Bruhah, when Papa at last stands back, rubbing his palms together, to show he concludes his examination. 'What is the patient's condition?'

'In my opinion . . . ' says Papa, 'as *Chief Veterinary Officer to The Kapital Zoo, with Special Responsibility for Large Mammals, chiefly Ungulates, particularly Elephants, both African and Indian*, the patient has arteriosclerosis, limiting the blood supply to his brain. We would expect him to suffer dizziness, poor memory, poor concentration, confusion, irrational outbursts, frustration, anger.

'Overlaying this chronic condition, he has recently suffered an acute ischemic event, such as is commonly termed a *minor stroke* . . . due to a small blood clot or a bleed in his brain.

'He seems to have stabilised, and may be out of immediate danger . . . but there is the perpetual risk of a recurrence, probably more severe, perpetually life-threatening. There is a need for sedation and immediate rest . . . he should avoid any work and stress . . . If the patient were an elephant of advanced years, I would say the prognosis is poor, and that we should expect a further crisis. But as he is a human being, I cannot be sure. The morbidity pattern is species-specific . . . But it is certain he must abstain *absolutely* from tobacco and alcohol . . . '

At this remark, the patient flicks open his eyes wide and glares up at Papa. It is as if he has been listening all along. And doesn't like to be told what to do, or instructed to abstain from his pleasures.

The Sick-Man finds his voice. And what he says is sudden, fast, fluent and vulgar.

Papa, himself, always shuns bad language. Not just because it is ugly to the ear. But because it is inexact, illogical and repetitive. Also unfriendly, uncomradely, un-Socialist and non-progressive. Plus an insult to the human spirit.

He says cursing always retards history, rather than advancing humanity, and always makes more enemies than friends.

Papa says you only have to translate swearing into normal language to see how little sense there is in it. And how unscientific it all becomes.

I don't recall all the bad words, and worse words that the patient uses. And in what order. Besides, there are some I'd never heard before. So I can only guess the meaning. But it's a sorry bundle of remarks, all tied together by lies and meanness —

'I am intimate with your mother, by her slack rear entry.'

'She sells her body in railway stations.'

'Her private parts are well known, from Minsk to Smolensk.'

'Her vagina is more capacious than Krubera Cave.'

Forgive my loose translations.

His remarks are exaggerations or complete untruths. I think he's saying hurtful things just to insult poor Papa.

He is talking of our dear Granny Anya, and not in a way that we — her family — remember her.

Papa just widens his eyes and gulps.

The patient continues, growling —

'And I don't know you from a pig's arsehole ... What kind of goat-fucking, sheep-humping retard are you, anyway?'

I can see Papa is surprised by the harsh, accusing turn the consultation has taken. But when you work in a zoo, with elephants, hippos and rhinos, you get used to your patients showing massive ingratitude, and throwing spontaneous tantrums on a huge scale.

So Papa remains composed. He announces his name, patronymic, rank and veterinarian specialism, but he is turned oddly pale and speaks with a stammering hesitancy. To which the patient replies —

'*Go back to the farmyard, Quack, I'll take a second opinion.*'

The patient has turned his gaze from Papa, sideways on Maybe-Bruhah.

'See to it, Lev. You *donkey's dribbling arsehole.*'

So the patient says. I rephrase, and drop some terms, to avoid offence. But you can probably still catch his drift.

'Koba,' says Bruhah, 'any other medical man will say the same.'

'He implies I am not fit to govern. The insolent Cosmopolitan, Zionist quack . . . '

'No, Koba. He says you have suffered an attack. So you need rest.'

Then the patient twists his head to take me in. He stares long, then frowns.

'What are you smiling at? Are you an imbecile?'

I shrug. I sniff.

'Is he a sprite?' the Sick-Man demands. 'Is he a *Leshi*?'

As it turns out, this is an unkind remark, because, as I happen to know, from the stories Papa read to me at bedtime when I was younger, Leshi are shape-shifting wood-sprites. They capture people, carry them back to their cave, then tickle them to death.

The only way to defend yourself against a Leshi is to turn all your clothes inside out, and wear your shoes on the wrong feet.

I protest. I say I am Yuri Zipit and that, appearances apart, I am a normal, terrestrial being, of the human species, aged twelve and a bit.

He nods. He winks, and taps the side of his nose confidentially.

'Don't worry,' he tells me, gesturing to the others, 'you can tell me everything shortly. These are only *Temporary, Unnecessary People*. I can make them disappear. I can *disinvent* them, whenever I wish. Or send them to work in a mine in The Cold Lands.'

'But, Koba . . . ' says Bruhah.

'*Go fuck yourselves* . . . ' the patient invites.

He winks at me again. But his friendship seems a dark, scary place. I'm not sure I want to enter in.

'Koba . . . ' Bruhah urges. 'You need rest.'

'The boy will stay with me. He can fetch me what I want. He will see to my needs.'

I see Papa's backward glance from the door as he is bustled out. His face is white as a dumpling. He wears an expression of hopelessness and sheer terror. He hoists a single vertical finger in front of his lips.

It's a secret code. But I know exactly what he means to tell me.

Shhh . . .

Mind your mouth. Don't slouch. These are grave times. Be warned. Pay close attention. Stop gibbering like a demented gibbon. Mind your manners. Stay on your guard. Don't confide in strangers. Change your underpants. Keep your lips sealed. If people ask you awkward questions, act simple-minded. Go to the lavatory when you can. You don't know when the chance will come again. Don't prattle on like a total idiot. Above all, don't mention politics, or voice opinions off the top of your head.

4

Comrade Elephant

So, there we are. Alone together. Just the two of us. Comrade Elephant and myself. In a small room. In the dead of night. Facing each other. In silence.

And, while I gather he must be a big and important beast, I can't be sure who he is exactly. We haven't been properly introduced. At the zoo, at least, he would bear some instructive sign or label.

Shango, Elephant — *Loxodonta* *africana***: Order —** *Proboscidea***: Do not feed: On no account attempt to touch.**

Questions are jostling to get asked in a hurry, elbowing each other in my mind, wrestling to come out first. Then, the pressure builds up, so they all squirt out in a loud, messy rush —
'Do you know you're dying, old man?'
'Why are your cheeks so scabby?'
'How did you smash up your arm?'
'Does no one ever answer you back?'

'Do you happen to know where my Papa has gone?'

But the sick-fellow is deaf to my curiosities. He simply ignores every question I ask. He only has a mind for his own concerns.

'Shhh . . . ' he says. 'Idiot child . . . ' And scowls as he swats the air, as if my words are an unpleasant smell he could simply waft away.

His look reminds me of an Iguana lizard. The head stays still. It betrays no emotion. The only feeling shows in the slow, dull, dark brown eyes that follow your movements precisely, like a predator, without warmth or pity.

His tone is gruff. He barks strict instructions, concerning his comforts. He is brisk, needy and ungrateful. You can tell he's used to getting his own way and having folk bend to his will. He seems to think I'm here just to do his bidding and benefit him.

He has me plump his pillows and lay the blanket over his legs. He has me fetch his pipe and a box of cigarettes from the desk. He wants water pouring into one glass, and vodka decanted into another.

He insists to know if the seals are unbroken on the bottles. Is the cellophane wrapping intact on the packet of cigarettes?

He wants me to taste from the glass before

he will drink. He wants me to lay out the pieces on the draughts board. He selects the white piece for himself.

'I suppose everyone tells you,' I say, 'that you look in some ways like Comrade Iron-Man . . . '

'There is a facial resemblance.' He smiles a quick, tight smile, then promptly stifles it, so the impression of friendliness is just a brief visitor, and slides right off the far side of his face.

'Yes. But many differences too . . . ' I say.

'Differences?' He frowns. 'What differences are those?'

'Don't take offence,' I say, 'but Comrade Iron-Man is a big man. A *handsome* man. He is a tall, straight-backed man. He is younger. His hair is dark, not silver. His skin is smooth and flat. But you are an old man. You are short. You have scabs on your cheeks . . . '

'Are you some expert on Comrade Iron-Man? Do you know more about him than *me*?'

'Not an expert, exactly,' I say, 'but I notice things. I have seen the photos, the posters, the newsreels. And I hear people talk about him.'

'And what do they say?'

'No one has a bad word,' I say. 'Not in public. Some people seem to love him. And the rest are scared of being shot, or sent to the camps. Everyone's too terrified to talk.

It's suicide to tell the truth.'

The Sick-Man does not welcome these comments. He does something twitchy with his nostrils. He raises his brows, narrows his eyes and regards me steadily, getting to make me feel small, trying to make me blink first.

He says that I misunderstand. Comrade Iron-Man is an idea, not a man. An inspiration. Not a simple, single person. He is a beacon to the people. He is a political necessity. He can be all possible things — younger or older, taller or shorter. He can be kind or stern. Harsh or forgiving. Old and wise or younger and vigorous. It depends on the circumstances and political needs of the time.

He says Comrade Iron-Man is a complexity that cannot be bound by biology or convention, or caged by a single body.

'Yes, they say it can't be easy for Comrade Iron-Man,' I agree. 'Everyone is scared of him. People are afraid to tell him the truth. And he is only human, after all. He gets used to getting his own way. And it is not his fault if people do such bad things in his name. They say there have been times in history when it's been safe to speak. But now is not one of them . . . '

'People who say such things are loose-tongued fools with a death-wish,' says the

Sick-Man. 'And you are a certifiable idiot.'

'Yes, sir, and no, sir,' I explain. 'It's true I've a *damaged mind*. It's a medical condition. But it doesn't make me a fool.'

I tell him about my accident and how it touches upon my mind. I lean forward so he can see, through my Pioneers' crew-cut, to the long ridge of scar on my cranium, and I show him my twisted arm.

'That's nothing ... Look here ... ' He rolls up the sleeve of his night-shirt to show his bent left arm. 'As a child, I was hit by a horse-drawn carriage.'

'Yes,' I say, 'the same. The same. I was hit by a horse-drawn milk cart, then by an electrical tram.'

Clearly, we have much in common, the Sick-Man and I.

'Were you ever struck by lightning, like me? On Sparrow Hills? What is your favourite colour?' I ask. 'Do you have a lucky number? And what is your football team? Do you have a favourite rodent?'

He just grunts. If he has any strong preferences in these regards, he isn't telling.

'Why are you sad?' I ask.

'Me? I'm not sad.' He sounds gruff. He frowns as if taken aback. He wipes the glistening corner of a moist eye. 'Not me.'

'There's sadness,' I say, 'here in this room.

'Thick. All around.'

'There is?' He looks over his shoulder, as if concerned.

'Thick, smoky, choking sadness. It clogs your breath. It makes me cough. And I feel there must have been many deaths around you . . . '

This is my intuition. You see, sometimes I know things about people, without knowing how I know them.

'It's true,' he concedes. 'Many are gone . . . passed on before me . . . Comrades, family, friends . . . '

He stares me full in the face.

'You are an odd child,' he says, softening. 'You have a strange face . . . A kind look . . . '

Then, I feel it happening again.

Out of the blue, as if a switch has been flicked, he starts, like all the others, telling me things — personal, secret, unnecessary things — things I'd rather not hear.

As usual, it starts badly. And then gets worse.

He sounds in a very dark, thoughtful mood.

'They say I killed Comrade Lenin,' he begins.

'They do?' I'm over twelve years old, but I'd never heard that one before.

'They said I poisoned him when I gave him his injections.'

'Oh?'

'For syphilis. Because he opposed my election as General Secretary.'

'Yes?'

'To get him out of the way. To give him a massive stroke. But I never did.'

'Good,' I say. 'Good.'

'And they say I killed my wife . . . '

'Yes?' I ask. 'They do?'

'But I did not kill my wife.'

'No?' I say. 'That's good.'

'I did not shoot her.'

'No?'

'She shot herself.'

'Why so?' I ask. After all, when people take the trouble to tell you these unnecessary, personal things, they expect you to cobble a concern.

'Just to spite me.' He shakes his head at the meanness of wives.

'Oh,' I nod. As if it all makes sense to me.

'My son, Arkady, tried to shoot himself too.'

'That's a shame,' I say.

'But he missed. More than once. Just grazing his temple.'

'Good,' I say, but it turns out this is a very poor, ill-considered answer.

'Good?' he sneers. He imitates me with a high-pitched tone. 'Good? How is it *good*? To miss shooting yourself? Twice? With a pistol?

From a distance of five centimetres?'

'I don't know,' I have to admit. Put like that, it does seem aimless or insincere.

'My life has been blighted by selfish relatives. They think they can get my attention, just by shooting themselves.'

'They do?'

'They try to kill themselves just to spite me. And succeed when I'd rather they fail. And fail when I'd prefer they succeed.'

'I'm sorry . . . ' I console.

'And I've been utterly shamed by useless sons . . . '

'Useless?'

'Arkady gets captured by the Germans. They offer to swap him for one of their generals we've caught. Of course, I say 'No'.'

'Why?'

'Why would I make such a swap? Giving something of value for something worthless? A great warrior for some useless relative, with only sentimental value?'

'Oh.'

'Then my other son, Viktor, does something beyond stupidity. He loses something important that isn't his to lose.'

'Important?'

'The National Ice-hockey Team.'

'Loses them?'

'He orders their plane to fly off in a

snowstorm. Of course, it crashes on take-off. Everyone's killed . . . '

'That's a shame,' I say.

'He never tells me. He thinks to hide it from me. He just picks another team to play in their place.'

'Oh.'

'Viktor,' I tell him, 'you are beyond hopeless. You are worse than useless. I give you one last warning. And never, ever, lose the National Team again . . . They are the world champions. It is the sport of the Motherland. Ice-hockey players like those don't grow on bushes.'

'Did he change his ways?'

'Yes. He's transformed himself into a hopeless drunk.'

'Do you have any daughters?'

'I have a daughter,' he concedes, 'called Nadezhda. She is sweet-natured, useless and soft in the head. She is a *horizontalist*. She spreads her legs for conmen and Zionists. She wants the world to lie on her belly. She wants to have babies by the enemies of the State.'

'Yes?'

Sometimes, in the face of a long disclosure, it is enough just to say 'Oh', 'Yes?', 'No?', 'Really?', or 'Is that so?', or 'You don't say.'

'Why am I telling you all this?' he demands, as if I'm to blame for his ugly, needless confessions.

'I have this effect.' I confess it. 'People tell me things . . . even though I never ask them . . . and don't want to hear. Aunt Natascha says I could be an interrogator for State Security. If they only cared for the truth . . . '

The Sick-Man reaches out, plucks three Herzegovina Flor cigarettes from the pack and rips them open, scrunches them in his palm, discarding the paper and cardboard tube, tamping the tobacco into the bowl of his pipe. Then he lights up.

I sense he resents me now, for loosening his secrets, and touching upon his pain.

'Idiot boy,' he mutters, under his breath.

'Me, sir?'

'You are a simpleton. You are very stupid. They must call you mean names at school . . . ' the Sick-Man says. 'Like *Moron, Idiotnik, Arse-wipe* and *Cretin?*'

'Yes,' I admit it, 'they mostly call me *Retard, Snot-Face* and *Yuri-Shat-His-Pants*. But when I first join Boris Tiverzin tells the rest of the class that I'm a biology experiment, made of bits of dead animal from my father's zoo, all sewed together, then brought to life by a lightning bolt . . . But, actually, this isn't even half-way true . . . '

I explain how it is to the Sick-Man.

Because I was run over by a milk truck,

and then by a tram, and as a toddler I once climbed through the bars into a cage to play with the Siberian tigers, and scratch their bellies, and ride on their backs, but never got hurt, and fell off a roof, but into a passing trailer loaded with straw and elephant dung, which broke my fall, and then got struck by lightning on Sparrow Hills, which made my hair stand up on end for months, Papa used to call me his *Koschei, The Deathless*, after the character in the fairy stories who could never be killed because he kept his soul apart from his body, inside a needle, in an egg, in a duck, which is inside a hare, which is inside a crystal chest, which is buried beneath an oak, on a deserted island, in the middle of the ocean.

And it always made me feel protected, so that although I got damaged I was always guarded and in some ways special.

The Sick-Man nods. He understands.

'Once, long ago, they used to call me *Scab-Face*,' he says. 'But they do not call me that any more. They used to laugh at me. But they don't laugh at me now . . . '

'I suppose not,' I agree.

'Enough futile recollections.' He taps the draughts board with the tip of his pipe. 'Now, we shall play Shaski.'

Soon we are sunk in our game, wrapped in

a cloud of tarry grey tobacco smog.

'You shouldn't smoke,' I warn him. 'Not when you're half-dead already.'

'No?'

'Papa says it gives you smoky lungs . . . excites the blood and alarms your heart. Plus you should keep your draughts on the back row as long as you can.'

He just grunts.

'Are you good at this game?' I ask. 'Do you have any strategy? Do you think many moves ahead?'

'Shhh,' he growls. He holds a finger to his lips, like Papa.

'I am a good player, myself,' I explain. 'I have vision. I have tactics. So, you mustn't mind losing to me, even though I'm a child with a damaged mind.'

He grunts. He mutters. If I beat him he will eat his feet. Both feet, he says. With horseradish dumplings. To me, this sounds a rash offer. We both look to his naked feet, laid up on the sofa. They are white, moist and pudgy, like newly made pastry. Some of his toes are joined, webbed like a duck's foot.

Even now, after only five moves each, I can see he is approaching *zugzwang*. So he can only move to his own disadvantage. He must advance. But he can only move in front of my piece. Then, because of his careless spacing, I can promptly jump four pieces of his.

He reaches out to move his piece. Then he hesitates. Then he frowns. Then a sly smile forms on his face.

'Now, I will invoke the *Counter-Reactionary Defence*,' he says, banging the tabletop with his closed fist. Clearly, he thinks he has me beaten.

'The *what*?' I say.

'The *Counter-Reactionary Defence* allows me to defend myself against liberal parasites and reactionary back-sliders. I can advance, and then capture, your leading, right-wing piece, if no effort has been made to correct its backward-looking tendencies, by moving it leftwards, in your past three moves.'

'I never knew,' I confess. I never saw it coming. In fact, I never knew this rule existed.

'Did you think you could loiter on the right with impunity? Now . . . ' He pounces. 'I can take two of yours.'

He jumps my piece. Then he jumps another piece. But I swear they were not at hazard before the *Counter-Reactionary Defence* came into force.

This way, he gets to the end of the board and wins a king-piece. So, now he can zigzag back and forth, picking off my men, one by one, or two by two.

'Your position is hopeless,' he says. 'You

were careless. You left your flank exposed, defended only by feeble, reactionary forces. But don't be disheartened . . . I am a strong player. I see new possibilities that others only guess at.'

We play some more. I am two men ahead in the second game, but he suddenly turns things round for himself, with the help of the *Usual-Suspects Gambit*, which is another new rule I know nothing about.

'It allows me to imprison all your men that have formed together in the manner of a demonstration or illegal gathering,' he explains. 'It is standard police practice. It is social hygiene, for the good of us all.'

And then he wins the third game with the *Common-Good Principle*, which enables him to exile, Far North of the board, any of my pieces that threaten the well-being of the majority, by being *enemies of the people*.

I am dismayed. I've always thought of draughts as a simple game of few rules. It is daunting to keep meeting these new political regulations I've never dreamed of.

'Don't be disappointed,' he says. 'Shaski is practical politics. Nobody has beaten me at this game for a long, long time.'

'How long?'

He frowns to consider. 'Twenty-seven years, I believe.'

'I'm not surprised,' I say. 'If you make up the rules as you go along . . . '

We sit in silence for a while.

When at last he speaks, it is to ask me if I like moving-pictures.

'Oh, yes,' I say, 'I love the movies.'

He tells me this is a good, correct, Socialist answer. Movies are the most progressive forms of art. Books are liberal. Novels waste time, loitering inside the head of small, petit-bourgeois characters. They examine the trivial thoughts and inconsequential feelings of unnecessary people.

'This boy has a sore conscience, this girl wants to visit The Kapital and marry a count. That man wants to scratch his itch . . . ' he says. 'But, we do not care about a man with an itch. We do not give a shit if he scratches . . . Stavrogin can go hang himself. Oblomov can stay in bed, for all I care. Pechorin can eat his horse. Anna Karenina can take in washing.'

'Yes?'

'We want what matters. We want to see the true events of history. The battle between the classes. The conflict of Labour and Kapital. Thesis, antithesis, synthesis . . . Maybe we are interested in the individual if he is a type, a man of his time, or a man in the eye of the conflict, or he is a great man who leads his people. And all this we can see in film. The action, the conflict, the groups, the peoples, as if we are watching history . . . '

He goes on about the foreign films that were captured during the war. Many German. Many Amerikan. Many from the film library of Joseph Goebbels himself, fellow film-lover and cohort of Hitler.

He asks me if I have watched the films of the great Communistic actor Charles Chaplin who represents the genius of the common person, playing him as a tramp, a worker, a poet and a dreamer. And who shows the cruelty of Kapitalism, and the posturing of dictators, and that life is a tragedy in close-up, but a komedy in long-shot. And that life is ruthless. So, to cope with it, you must be ruthless yourself . . .

I say I have not seen the films of Comrade Chaplin. Because we only see Homeland films in our Picture House. But I have been fortunate enough to have watched *The Humpbacked Horse, The Fall of Berlin, The Symphony of Life* and *How the Heroic Workers of Novomoskovsk Achieve Their Five Year Collective Construction Targets Two Years Ahead of Plan.*

'You've never watched Amerikan *Western* movies?' he asks.

'What?'

'Cowboy films. With Indians, bows and arrows, spitting, scalping, horses and shooting.'

I shrug. These things are not within my experience.

'You should. These are an education. The Amerikan Western shows the moral emptiness, the lawlessness of Kapitalist Culture . . . Amerika is a wasteland, a tundra or desert. Every man carries a gun. Often there is only a single, powerful man to bring order from the chaos, or to protect the working people.

'There are Tsars ruling Business. Kulaks controlling the land. The Cossacks are their henchmen.

'The good characters wear light-coloured clothes, the bad characters wear dark. There is no art, no culture. So they just drink whisky, play poker and visit prostitutes. All the time they fight each other, because there is no Socialist-Solidarity or Class-Unity.

'You know there will be a fight when the camera moves from one face to another and back again. When the camera freezes on the face, they are preparing to shoot.'

'Yes?'

'The greatest Western film is *Stagecoach*. It is directed by the great *John Ford*. And the greatest cowboy actors are *Spencer Tracy* and *Clark Gable*.

'But there is an odious cowboy actor called

John *Wayne* who has appointed himself as an enemy of the proletariat, always mocking Socialism and decrying the achievements of the Socialist Union. So, we will not be surprised if some patriotic soldier of the Union of Socialist Republics will go someday soon to Amerika and knock on the door of his home — at 4750 Louise Avenue, Beverly Hills — to silence him, once and for all, with a knife through his heart, ice-axe through the temple, or stiletto into his spine . . . '

★ ★ ★

I look around the room. I wander to the easel bearing the large map of our great and wide, beloved Homeland.

There are maybe twenty pins with titchy, triangular flags attached — red, white and blue — spreading South and East of The Kapital, and also up into The Cold Lands.

The Sick-Man follows my gaze. 'We must find a new place for the Rootless, Zionist Cosmopolitans,' he explains.

'New towns?'

'Camps.'

'Holiday camps?' I ask. 'For recreation? With swimming pools, football pitches and running tracks. Like those for Junior Pioneers?'

'Work camps,' he says. 'For hard work. And harder work.'

'*Rootless Cosmopolitans?*' I ask. 'Are they the Gypsies and tramps and refugees?'

I guess he is planning new houses and new jobs for the homeless.

'*The Jews*,' he says. 'They want to leave their Motherland. They want a home in Palestine. They always look to the Amerikans as their friends.'

'Papa's friend Pyotor Kolganov teaches me the piano. He's Jewish. But he's not rootless. He likes living in The Kapital. He's on the third floor of his building. He said he could never move. It would be too difficult to shift the grand piano down the stairwell . . . '

'There are Jews and Jews . . . ' the Sick-Man says. He taps his nose. 'There are many Jewish killers in white coats, under the mask of *Professor-Doctors*, who plot to murder our leadership. And there are many Jewish Nationalists who are spies, agents of Amerikan Intelligence.'

'Aunt Natascha's friend Vasili is Jewish too. But he's not a Spy or Killer-Doctor. He's an attendant in a lunatic asylum.'

The Sick-Man looks away, adrift in his thoughts. I don't think he's interested in my opinions, or considering contrary views.

'How are you going to tell them all apart?'

I ask. 'The spies and the cobblers, the killers and the poets?'

The Sick-Man turns his dark, hooded eyes on me. The dark pupils have no sheen or sparkle. They swallow light and give nothing back.

'It is not necessary to tell them apart,' he growls. He shrugs.

'No?'

'No man, no problem,' he says. 'Death solves everything.'

'Yes?'

Sometimes he talks in riddles. So, there's no guessing what he means, or what cloudy thoughts swirl round in his head.

'I have taken to you,' says the Sick-Man. 'You have a soothing smile and a kind heart. You remind me of my dead son Arkady.'

'I do?'

'You are passably clever. And yet dismally stupid. You aim to please but you lack ambition. You have no guile. People trust you. It's a rare combination. And there is something calming and comforting about your presence. Would you like to make yourself useful?'

'Thank you, Comrade,' I say. 'I would.'

'Then, I will appoint you to a position, here, in my household.'

'A position?'

'A vacancy has arisen.'

'Sir?'

'It is an important position. You will be my *Food-Taster, Technician First Class.*'

'Yes, sir?' I ask. 'What would I do?'

'You taste all my food before me. And sip all my drinks. Just to check they are fit for me to consume. Ensure they haven't been tampered with.'

'Is this a new position?' I ask.

'I had a food-taster before . . . ' he concedes. 'And one before that . . . And one before that. But none of them stuck to the task . . . '

'No?'

'They were all allergic to toxins. Each in his different way. One was sensitive to strychnine. And another was allergic to cyanide.'

I consider the offer. I consider it from all angles. I like food. I like it very much. And there are worse jobs than eating the same fine foods as top-rank personages, such as Marshals, Deputies, Ministers, General Secretaries and Ambassadors. And I'd always dreamed I would, one day, overcome my challenges to hold a post of importance. Besides, I sense, refusal is not an option.

'I will eat for you and the Motherland like a patriotic Slav,' I say.

'You will have the freedom of the building. But you will make yourself available as and when I require, at breakfast, lunch and supper . . .

'Also you can report back to me whatever is said in my house. You will join the Special Security Section. In particular you will listen out for whatever is said behind my back by Comrade Bruhah, Marshal Krushka, Deputy Bulgirov and Secretary Malarkov.'

'Yes?'

'They attend in the evenings. They hang around. They take supper with me. They pass themselves off as friends. They are easy to recognise. I call them *the hyena, the pig, the donkey* and *the goat* . . . They are not so clever as they think. They will speak freely in front of you, because you are a fool and a child . . . They will assume you can't understand what they say, or decipher what they mean . . . '

He reaches to the desk. He scribbles on a sheet of paper, a note in spidery green ink and passes it to me. It reads —

The bearer is my personal food-taster.
Technician First Class, Yuri Zipit.
Be advised. He is a harmless moron.
Afford him every assistance he requires.
He has the freedom of the house.

Help him and you help me.
Thwart him and you thwart me.

Josef Petrovich
General Secretary

'Go now,' he says, 'I will sleep. And if Bruhah asks you what we spoke about and he surely will — be warned — tell him I talked about the *Mingrelian Conspiracy*.'

'Will he understand?'

'He will, indeed,' says the Sick-Man, 'because he, *himself*, is the Mingrelian Conspirator.'

'Really?' I say.

But there's no answer.

The Sick-Man's eyes have already closed. He snorts, then begins a slow rumbling snore, so I turn away, walk to the door. I let myself out.

Now I must go and find Papa and tell him the good news. Though I must not seem to brag.

I walk out with pride. For I came into this room as a nobody, and left as a *somebody*, as a person of standing, as a Food-Taster, Technician First Class, to the General Secretary of something-or-other, who is a man of some importance, well connected in the Party.

5

The Four Iron-Men

Comrade Bruhah is leaning against the wall at the end of the corridor. Then he's striding towards me. Fast and furious. I suppose he's been waiting for me to emerge from the Sick-Man's room. He wears a poisonous frown on his puffy yellow face, like a cane toad (*Rhinella marina*).

'Have you seen my Papa?' I say.

Bruhah ignores this. He lays a stern, stiff arm on my shoulders. Well, in truth, it's more like a headlock, with his arm circling my neck. I feel like I'm back at breaktime in school, bullied all over again.

'Why do you smile all the time?' he snaps. 'Do you think the world's a pleasant place? Do you think I'm here to be kind to you? Do you think everyone's your friend?'

He drags me along. I'm bent like a hinge. He stoops and presses his shiny, warm face close to mine. I can smell peppermint, vodka and onions, and a hint of musky perfume besides, as if he'd been rubbing against something more fragrant than himself, most likely a woman.

'The Comrade likes you, you shitty, little, maimed runt,' he says. 'Why on earth would that be?' He looks to his watch. 'You've been with him for *four hours*.'

'We play draughts . . . We swap stories . . . We share memories . . . ' I say. I am gasping because the Marshal is pressing the air from my neck. 'We have things in common . . . '

'You do?'

'We both have a gammy arm. His mother went missing, like mine. He got called names at school, like me . . . '

'You have his confidence?' Bruhah steps back, releasing my neck. He looks bemused. 'He tells you things? *Personal, private things?*'

'Yes.'

I tell him of my appointment. I say I am to be the Boss's food-taster. First Class. And, if necessary, to die to save him for the Motherland.

'The Comrade is not himself, these days. He is sick,' says Bruhah. 'In his head. We must not take advantage of his good nature. We must help him as much as we can. So you must make me a promise.'

'Comrade?'

'Listen carefully to whatever he says. Everything. And report it back to me. Nothing is too big to tell. Nothing is too small.

'Yes?'

'And, in return, I will look after you.'

'Thank you,' I say.

'You will need looking after,' he says. 'You will need it very badly.'

'I will?' I ask. I had no idea.

'Close your eyes,' he commands, 'and think of the best that could happen to you . . . '

Yes. I see it now. I've returned home from school. But there are three suitcases in the hall, not two. Mama is returned to us, out of the blue. I hear her shriek and giggle and Papa's deep laughter.

'Now,' Bruhah pinches my shoulder, 'think of the worst thing that can happen . . . '

I wince. As before, I return to the apartment. But in this imaginary scene there is only one suitcase. Yes, Papa has been taken from me. Who knows where.

'I know exactly what you're thinking,' the Marshal tells me. 'Every last detail. I can read your shallow child's mind. But you have not thought hard enough, because I can make the worst far worse, and I can make the best even better . . . '

'You can?'

'That is my business. Making a person's life better, or unbearably bad, depending on what he deserves.'

'Oh.'

72

'So anything is possible for you, Yuri, you foul-smelling dollop of shit. The best and the worst, North of Hell, and South of Heaven, and all points in between. You must simply do as I say.'

'I must?'

'Do you know what I do in life?'

'No.' I admit it.

'I am an artist. But where a painter uses colours and a potter uses clay, I use pain and fear. For I am a terrorist.'

'You are?'

'I terrify people. I arrest them. I punish them. I break them. I crush their bones. I pop their eyes. I shred their souls . . . '

'Ouch,' I say.

'Sometimes they kill themselves before I can start. They drop dead of fear before I have a chance to lay a finger on them. But I do not get other people to do my dirty work.'

'No?'

'If a man needs shooting, I do it myself. If a man needs his finger nails pulling off, or his eyes popping out, or his bollocks kicking off, I do it myself. I do it for the Motherland. I do it for Socialism. And I do it for my own satisfaction, as a job well done.'

Of course, I don't believe him. He's just playing around, trying to scare me. Nobody would deliberately hurt another person. Not

73

in those needless, ugly, cruel ways.

Papa says most hurt is unthinking — inflicted when people are not vigilant enough to the other person's feeling, and act without kindness, and without first considering the consequences.

'Stand still,' says Bruhah. 'Now observe how it is . . . ' He smiles. He slides finger and thumb either side of my nose. It tickles, until he tightens his grip, then gives a sharp jerk, with a twist.

It is an evil conjuring trick. There is the screech of a branch being bent. Then a sharp snap, like a twig underfoot, which echoes through all the bones of my skull. It feels like a bolt of lightning has passed through my face. Golden flashes spark out in all directions. I want to retch. I feel a hot spray of blood in the back of my throat.

I slump against the wall. I think I pass out for some seconds.

'That's your nose,' he points out. 'It was whole . . . but now it is broken.'

'Aaah,' I say. Blood is trickling over my lips, and down my front.

'Understand. The whole of your body is like this.'

'Ugh?' I sniff warm clots of myself down my nose, into my mouth, then swallow.

'Everything whole can be broken, inside

and out. Skull, liver, teeth, heart, spirit. And, with each break comes more pain . . . worse pain . . . But that was nothing. It was only your nose. So it doesn't matter . . . '

He releases me. He pats me on the shoulder and smiles. 'That was a tiny thing compared to what I could do to you, if I wanted to hurt you properly, like an artist . . . '

'No need,' I protest.

'So, you will tell me whatever the patient says to you.'

'Yes,' I sniff.

'When you talk to the Comrade, there is a right way and a wrong way to do it.'

'Sir?' I've lifted the end of my shirt to my nostrils to block the drip of blood down my front.

'Look him in the eye. But don't look at him too long in the eye . . . Always tell him the truth. But don't tell him too much truth . . . Do not show any weakness. He despises the weak. But you should not show strength either. It will make him ill at ease. Say whatever you want, by all means. As long as it's what he wants to hear. Do you understand me?'

'Yes, sir.' I sniff hard and then swallow warm globs of my blood.

'Good,' he says, 'I think we are going to be

very good friends. Here, I think you deserve a prize . . . ' He reaches into his pocket and hands me a thin strip of silver foil. 'I give you this because I am a kind man who loves children . . . '

I sniff. 'Thank you, sir. What is it?'

'It is called *chewing gum*,' he says. 'It is a gum. For chewing. So it goes in your mouth. It comes from Amerika. It is called *Wrigley's Spearmint*. You are very fortunate. You slither of shit. There are only seven packets in the entire Socialist Union.'

Although Marshal Bruhah is very rude and a hurtful nose-breaker, I realise this must be because he is an unhappy person and has many worries in his life, perhaps with special responsibilities, annual accounts, agendas, paperwork, troubles and difficulties, such as make Papa tetchy too.

Papa always told me, 'Everyone has their reasons, Yuri. So, if you don't understand someone's actions, you simply haven't understood their mood, their character and situation . . . '

'Thank you, sir,' I say. I let my mouth play around with it, and my teeth sink into this strange grey, gummy thing, which passes for a delicacy in Amerika. ' . . . It's very chewy. And very minty . . . '

And yet oddly hard to swallow.

'Come,' he says, 'I lack a mother's kind touch. Matryona, here, will look after you even better than I can . . . '

★ ★ ★

Matryona is the housekeeper, in a black sack of a dress with a white apron. She is plump and pink and smiley. She seems broader than she is tall.

'Oh, the poor, broken, bleeding boy,' she says and tousles my hair. 'And your poor, bleeding nose.' Then she hugs me. She squeezes my head into her hot bouncy, powdery bosom. Sunk deep in her musky flesh, my cheeks burn and I hear her heart like the close tick of a clock.

She says I will need my nose twisting back straight, and then cotton wool up each nostril. Then a bed. She says I can sleep with the others in the men's staff dormitory.

We climb a set of stairs to the first floor. We wander down a long corridor. We find a long darkened room arranged like a hospital ward, with low metal-framed beds around the walls, and a long table down the centre.

Five of the twelve beds are taken. I take the empty bed close to the door.

'Papa?' I whisper to the dark serenade of snores. But the dark gives up no reply. He'd answer if he was here. I will have to wait for the morning to find him.

I try to be positive. I think what Papa would say. That all will seem better next day. That a broken nose is better than a broken skull. That a dull throb is better than a screaming, shooting pain.

My head hits the pillow. I'm gone.

*   *   *

I am woken at seven by the chatter and clatter of the household rising. There is a chorus of coughing, spitting and bickering. There is the smell of warm, moist, leaky bodies. There's the stamp of boots on wooden boards.

I follow the staff down to the canteen to take my breakfast.

I look around for Papa but he is nowhere to be seen.

I am alone in their company. No one returns my looks or smiles. So I take a solitary seat at the side, at the end of a long pine refectory table.

I have been there a few minutes when a shadow falls across me and someone sits down beside me and lays a plate of floury, yeasty-smelling, steamy muffins on the table.

'Good morning, kid,' he says.

I turn to see the strangest sight. It is only

the spit of Comrade Josef Iron-Man, all over again.

But a different spit.

This is not the thin, sick, grey-haired Iron-Man I met the night before. This is a raven-haired, tall, thick-set, youngish Iron-Man with deep scarlet pits on his cheeks.

He extends a giant hand to shake mine.

'I am Felix,' he says.

'Yuri,' I say. 'Happy to meet you.'

'Tell me . . . ' he frowns, 'why do you keep them *there*, of all places?'

'Keep what?'

'Those hard-boiled duck eggs . . . '

'Pardon?'

'In your ears.'

'Excuse me . . . ' I say

'Here . . . ' He taps my right ear and produces a still-warm egg from his palm. 'And here . . . ' He touches my left ear and discovers a second egg. 'You know what would be best?' he says. 'Everything considered . . . '

'What?'

'I think we should eat them for breakfast with these hot buttered muffins.'

This sounds an excellent plan. To share my eggs and his muffins. We eat in satisfied silence. The egg yolks are rich as molten butter and golden as the sun.

Then another being joins us, parking himself on the bench opposite, which creaks under his lowered weight. I look up to see who it is.

Yes. Only another one. No lie.

Another Comrade Josef Iron-Man.

But a different-looking one. This one is stout, of middle years and middling tall. I am struck by his large, fleshy, cabbage-leaf ears.

'This is Rashid,' Felix tells me.

'Pleased to meet you, Comrade,' I say.

'Good morning, young rascal,' says Rashid. 'What brings you here?'

I tell them I came to help my father, a Professor of Veterinary Science. I say we became separated. I ask if they have come across him.

I describe him. I say he is a tall, absent-minded man, with a bald spot, a stoop and an astrakhan collar, and carries the scents of scorched wool and pipe tobacco. I explain he is especially clever, with a profound know-ledge of Cordate Neurology.

'I haven't seen him,' says Rashid. 'Cordate Neurology, you say?'

'Nor I,' says Felix. 'What was the purpose of your visit here?'

I say we came in a medical capacity, to treat a sick man who looks like . . .

Then I fall silent. I am loath to tell them.

80

For fear of causing offence. Or sounding rude. Or stating the obvious.

'Forgive me for saying so,' I explain, 'but the sick man looks like Comrade Iron-Man.'

'Yes?' asks Felix. 'What on earth do you mean, he *looks like Comrade Iron-Man?*' He seems bewildered by the notion. 'Are you suggesting he looks more like Comrade Iron-Man than me? Or Rashid, here?'

Both the Comrade Iron-Men look surprised. And hurt. That there might be a more Iron-Man-like Iron-Man than them. Big-Ears and Pock-Face exchange bemused glances.

Well, I don't want to cause offence. I want to answer politely. But it's hard to find the right words to tell people apart when they all look like Comrade Iron-Man, while they also look like themselves.

'Well, you both show a fine likeness to Comrade Iron-Man, to be sure . . . But he does too . . . ' I explain.

'How do you mean, exactly?'

'He had brushed back hair, like you both. And a moustache like you. And scars like Rashid. But smaller ears. And older-looking than both of you. And with a twisted left arm . . . '

'Did he talk?' asks Big-Ears.

'Yes,' I said. 'He sounded just like Comrade Iron-Man himself, when he's talking on the

81

radio. Except he used a lot of ugly, rude words.'

'A *talking* Comrade Iron-Man ... ' Big-Ears shakes his head. He whistles in awe.

'A *swearing* Comrade Iron-Man,' says Pock-Face, clearly bewildered by my news, 'who's had voice-training. And taken cussing-classes, and blasphemy lessons.'

'If they've taken on a new *Talker*,' says Big-Ears, 'who can swear like the Boss himself, there are repercussions all down the line, for *Statues* and *Mutes*, and the likes of us.'

'It stands to reason.'

'We're just *Walkers*, you see,' says Felix. 'And *Long-Standers* ... '

'And *Comers* and *Goers*,' says Rashid.

'Excuse me?' I say.

'We are doubles,' says one. 'For the Big Boss.'

'And triples, sometimes,' says the other. 'We stand in for him when he needs to be in different places, all at the same time. There are five of us, at present, all told.'

'So he can be in the Crimea, on affairs of State,' says Rashid, 'while we watch the tanks roll by for him, for hours on end, in some procession around Martyr Square while, at the same time, opening The Red Proletariat Printing Works in Novgorod.'

'Or supposing there's word that some foreign agent wants to take a pot-shot at the Boss. We can leave in the limousine at the front, and take the flack, or catch the bullet, while he slips safely out at the back.'

'Sometimes, when the Boss spends the day here at the dacha, we each repose in one of his sitting rooms. It is quite relaxing. We can sit in his chair, and read *Pharaoh* by Boleslaw Prus, which is one of his favourite books, or *The Combat History of the 2nd Guards Tank Army from Kursk to Berlin: Volume 1*, which is another. But he will not have us smoke his cigarettes, or drink his mineral water.'

'That way, if an assassin breaks in, he will not know who to shoot for the best. Or he'd be tricked into killing the wrong Comrade Iron-Man, which would be a great blessing for the Motherland.'

'But we aren't allowed to talk as the Boss, in case we say something wrong.'

'Once, a substitute-Boss drank too much at an embassy dinner, and got carried away. He made under-the-table approaches, of an intimate kind, to the wife of the Swedish Ambassador. Then he entered into a hasty, ill-considered treaty with the Amerikans . . . '

'A fatal mistake.' Rashid holds fingers to his temple as if firing a pistol.

'So, now, we're all sworn to silence,' says Felix. 'It's safer all round.'

'Well, this old man never stopped talking,' I say. 'He had a foul mouth. And he shouted at Marshal Bruhah. He called him a *donkey's arsehole*.'

Rashid raises his eyebrows. Felix frowns and rubs his chin. They eye me in silence.

'Do you know what, kid?' Felix says at last. 'I think you maybe met *Him*. The Boss himself.'

'So, he's really short, then, with foxy eyes?' I say. 'Smokes a pipe. And smells like a goat?'

'Beats me,' says Felix. 'To tell the truth, I've never met him.'

'Me neither,' says Rashid. 'But he passed me once on the staircase in the Palace of the People. At least, I think it was him, but you never know . . . It might have been another one of us . . . For we both saluted each other.'

'It's our job to *be* him, you see,' says Rashid, 'in his absence. Not pass the time of day with him.'

'He has more important things to do,' says Felix, 'than waste his time chattering with nobodies like us . . . '

'He has to look after his peoples,' says Rashid.

'He has fifteen Socialist Republics to govern,' says Felix, 'from Armenia to Uzbekistan.'

It makes me shiver. Looking back, if I'd known from the start that I was talking to the real Josef Iron-Man, I'd have been more careful what I said, and how I said it.

* * *

Enjoying the luxury of my boiled egg breakfast in the company of my two new friends, and two most favourite Comrade Iron-Men in the whole wide world, I was not surprised when we were interrupted by a man who introduced himself as Comrade Alexei Dikoy, Director at The Kapital Arts Theatre.

In appearance and clothing, he too resembled no one so much as the Great Father, Gardener of Human Happiness, Kind Uncle, Man of Iron, Comrade Josef Iron-Man himself.

He frowned down at me. He scowled at Rashid and Felix. He told them that they must make themselves ready to commence the day's training.

He said they would be employing the methodology of his personal friend and mentor, the deceased theatrical director Konstantin Sergeyevich Stanislavsky, may he rest in peace, the confidante of Anton Chekhov, Leo Tolstoy, Nicolai Gogol and Alexander Pushkin.

He said that they would use the staff recreation room as rehearsal space. He said they would commence in two and a half minutes. And that we should exit the green room immediately. He said they would have to draw on their *emotional memory* and the *lived truths* of their lives.

He said I should come too, and make myself available to fetch refreshments from the kitchen, and sweep the floor, and dog's-body as required. It did not occur to him that I might have a father to find, or any business other than serving him.

I asked him, in passing, if he had come across my Papa, Doctor Roman Alexandrovich Zipit, in his travels around the house.

'Who is he? This father of yours . . .'

'He is a vet. He is a famous Elephantologist.'

'Then I have not met him. The Theatrical and the Elephantastical are professions that rarely answer any urgent call to convene on common ground.'

'Shame,' I explained. 'It's just I've lost him.'

'How old is he?'

'Fifty-seven-and-three-quarters,' I said.

He nodded solemnly. 'Don't worry. The solution is in the age. Having reached this far in life, he shows a capacity to continue without you. He'll survive. He'll turn up. Relatives always do, whether you want them to or not.'

He gave me a downward expression of sympathy and patted my crown.

Of course, I followed in his wake, carrying a small samovar, as he'd instructed.

I have to say that of all the Iron-Men that I had met so far, Comrade Alexei Dikoy was the most commanding, natural and life-like, and much more realistic than the real thing, which seemed old, tired, grumpy, dirty, smelly and worn-down.

His walk was just like the Comrade Iron-Man we saw in the newsreels. His face wore a greatness and a calm. His presence was like a charge of electricity. It made the hairs rise on the back of my neck. I could hear the beat of my racing heart, throbbing in my ears.

He was an Iron-Man you would follow, barefoot through The Cold Lands, to the very gates of Hell.

'Come along, you towering dwarfs, you galumphing peasants . . . ' he barked at Felix and Rashid, 'today you will learn to play not a human being, but a *granite monument*.'

6

Immortality for Beginners

When your father is a Professor of Cordate Neurology, and entertains Academicians, and suffers writers, and keeps company with intellectuals, and is happy to hear actors spill their favourite stories all over again, and doesn't draw the line at artists, even though they're convinced the world owes them a living, then life becomes an education in itself, and there's a lot you learn just by listening to what is said around you, over your head, behind your back, through thin walls, and straight to your face.

For instance, this is a story I overhear Papa tell to Comrade Anna, Curator of Large Mammals —

There was an international competition for the best book about elephants.
France entered a lavishly illustrated volume called *The Sex-Lives of the Elephants*.
England presented a treatise called 'Elephants: a Business Model'.
Germany submitted a twenty-four

volume work entitled *The Theory and Praxis of Elephantology: an Introduction*.

The USA furnished one million copies of a leaflet for a prize-draw, 'Win an Elephant. No purchase necessary.'

Our Motherland sent three volumes, entitled —

Vol. 1: The Role of Elephants in the Great October Socialist Revolution.

Vol. 2: The Happy Life of Elephants Under the Progressive Socialist Constitution.

Vol. 3: The Union of Socialist Republics — Motherland of Elephants.

Papa also tells me about the sorry life of elephants in the USA and some of the worst crimes Amerikan history has committed against them.

He tells how Thomas Edison, the inventor, in 1903, electrocuted an elephant called Topsy at Luna Park, Coney Island, and filmed the murder to show in kinemas, to demonstrate the danger of the alternating current, so people would buy his competing version of electricity — the direct current — instead.

And Papa tells how in 1913, in Erwin, Tennessee, they gave a courtroom trial to an old elephant called Mary, after she had

89

defended herself against an attack by her cruel handler. And the jury found her guilty of murder. So, then, they executed her — hanging her, by hoisting her by the neck from a railway derrick.

★ ★ ★

But we don't just talk elephants, Papa and I. We have many other interests besides. We talk at length about zoos, supper, good manners, science and football too.

Papa tells me how Comrade Iron-Man himself took a deep interest in matters veterinarian, biological and experimental.

Papa tells me how his very own teacher, Professor Ilya Ivanovich Ivanov, had invented *artificial insemination*, which is a special way for animals to have sex — but with most of the pleasure taken out, and without even needing to touch each other.

And had then been awarded a grant, from the Politburo itself, with Comrade Iron-Man's personal approval, to create a new type of being, a human-primate hybrid. Because that way the Socialist Union could defend itself with a new army, an invincible fighting machine made up of soldiers who were half-monkey, half-human.

It was just a matter of finding the right

balance. Because the generals had seen how soldiers who were all-human could turn out timid, sensitive to pain, fearful, and fussy about food. While monkeys liked fighting and would eat any old rotten garbage for rations, but wouldn't take orders, wear berets, march in formation, care for their uniforms, salute officers, or take to military discipline.

So Professor Ivanov goes to Conakry, Guinea, to the Pasteur Institute, to put some tough monkey spirit into the soldier-mix, and soften their wild apishness with some human obedience.

First off, he tries to get female apes pregnant with human sperm. But it never seems to take. As if there's always some obstacle, or barrier.

So, Ivanov comes back to the Motherland to try the reverse procedure. He squirts the sperm from orangutans into Socialist women. But the beasts never succeed in getting any Socialist ladies pregnant, besides they didn't take to the Slav climate and diet, so they kept on dying carelessly. Even Ivanov's favourite, called Tarzan. And by the time he'd run out of orangutans, and monkey gizzum, he got arrested, then died of a stroke.

But Trofim Lysenko, who was head of Genetics at The Socialist Academy of Sciences, told Comrade Iron-Man you *could* teach plants and animals to enjoy the Slav weather. And that they would pass the lessons on to their offspring. Who would learn some more, and pass it on to their young too. So, eventually even coconut and pineapple and oranges could adapt to The Cold Lands, and learn to love the snow.

But, as it turned out, it was hard to teach plants they enjoyed sub-zero cold, and there were lots of bad harvests, year after year, without any vegetables learning much about The Cold Lands, or passing on a love of the freezing Motherland to their young.

★   ★   ★

In my class at school our Mathematics teacher — Professor Pavel Popov — is known to be strict. But I would not say he is a quarter as strict, nor half as sarcastic, as Comrade Theatrical Director Alexei Dikoy when he is attempting to teach Rashid and Felix to act like the Great Father, Josef Iron-Man.

'When I ask you to *walk* across the room like Comrade Iron-Man,' the Director barks at Felix, 'I do not ask a lot. In fact, I ask very little. But I do demand that you use your *emotional memory* and let it inform your *method of physical actions*. And I ask that you incorporate the *given circumstances* that we know about this character, Our Leader . . . '

Then the Director starts to discourse on the background circumstances that make Comrade Iron-Man walk as he does — that he is seventy-odd years old, that he comes from Georgia, that he has two toes joined together on his left foot, that his father was a cobbler, and his mother a housemaid, that he survives smallpox as a child and damages his left arm as a young man, that he attends the Tiflis Spiritual Academy, that he joins Comrade Lenin and the Bolsheviks, that his young wife bears him a son but then perishes of typhus, that he fights in the Revolution, that he then joins the Reds to fight the Whites, that he joins the provisional government . . .

And when you think the Director is quite finished giving Iron-Man's background for walking on his feet that way, he starts again on his *objective* and then on his *super-objective*. And what is his *through-line*? And what about the *magic-if*?

Above all, he demands that Felix and Rashid ask themselves the fundamental questions about the walking-complex —

Why does Iron-Man cross the room? *What is he saying* to the world, by crossing the room?

And in the end, having crossed the room,

what does he hope to *achieve* by it?

'Now, I ask you one more time. And I ask you politely. And I ask you patiently, in a spirit of Comradeship, as one artist to another . . . ' says Director Dikoy, 'cross the room like Comrade Iron-Man, but remember you are the Man of Iron, Leader of the Socialist World, that your Iron-Will has crushed Hitler . . . but that there is yet a tender side to your nature that includes a love of children, family, country, Mozart, particularly the later piano concertos, especially Number 21 in C Major, and literature, including the short stories of Chekhov, and most especially *The Lady with the Dog* . . . '

You can see that poor Felix is daunted and confused by all this information, and does not know quite how to use it for the best, to move his feet, because he steps on his untied bootlace on his way to tripping over the samovar.

'Stop. Stop,' the Director screams. 'Stop that dreadful *shuffling* and *stumbling* . . . ' He is holding his hands across his eyes, to avoid witnessing the travesty of Felix's movements.

'Sorry,' says Felix, lamely, picking himself up and dusting himself down.

'It is not your fault,' the Director admits. 'You are simply a peasant, a children's entertainer, a juggler from Yekaterinburg, with no more to offer than a face that fits . . . We are getting too far ahead of ourselves . . . You cannot move your arms properly. Not yet. You do not know how to work your legs. You have no balance. Your centre of gravity is skewed . . . And you do not understand how to carry your head . . . 'We will take things back to the very basics. First we will have to learn to *breathe* like Comrade Iron-Man . . .'

★   ★   ★

My first meal with the Boss is a breakfast. I am required to taste all the foods laid out. Then, if I am not sick within thirty minutes, he knows the meal may be free of toxins and safe to eat.

He sits at the desk in his living room. He nods to me, then returns his gaze to his papers. There is a typewritten list of names, several sheets long. Like a teacher correcting good homework, he is ticking each one, nodding. Sometimes smiling.

Breakfast is laid out on a small circular table. Much is familiar. I have no trouble dealing with the breads, porridges, yoghurts, cheeses, cold meats, nuts or dried fruit, but I do not know how to approach the long, curved, freckled, yellow vegetable. Whatever it is, it isn't Slavic.

It tapers at each end, with a black scar on the one side and a pale stalk on the other. It isn't clear which side to attack it from. So I just dive in and take a bite. The outside is fleshy and fibrous. It puts your teeth on edge. But the inside is a sweet soft pulp.

The Boss raises his eyes from his papers, watching my vigorous chewing and vain attempts to swallow.

'You peel it first.'

'Oh.'

'It's called a *banana*. It is my favourite fruit. Here. I will show you once. And only once.'

He plucks one from the bunch and reveals how to undress the thing, pulling the rind down the length of it, in three long strips, exposing the curved column of creamy white pulp inside.

He nibbles off the tip, chews, nods and swallows.

He's right. It is edible, providing you first discard the skin. In fact, the taste is not unpleasant.

Let nobody mislead you. It is no easy task, either, being Food-Taster, First Class, to Comrade Iron-Man, General Secretary of the Central Committee of the Communist Party of the Socialist Union.

Within a couple of days, I come to realise

that the Boss is an insomniac with a hearty appetite. There is a lot of eating to be done, all times of the day, never mind the drinking. The hours are not short, nor regular.

The main work of the day is usually between eleven at night and three in the morning, when the Boss takes a long, late dinner at the dacha, with his colleagues, Bruhah, Malarkov, Bulgirov and Krushka. There is drinking, leading to carousing. There may be forfeits, bets, wrestling, horse-play, pissing yourself, vomiting, falling over, fist-fighting, tumbling down stairs and breaking glass. It can go on until five or six in the morning.

Breakfast is a brief and simple meal taken any time in the morning. Then, a light lunch is taken at teatime.

A First Class, Food-Taster — as opposed to an Assistant-Taster, or Second Class Taster — must attend all three daily meals and sample every item of food and drink offered up for the Boss's sustenance and pleasure.

This is not a job for the faddy eater, since you must taste all and every food, whether it is to your taste or not. As a Georgian, Comrade Iron-Man is partial to many local dishes from his homeland that involve aubergine, walnuts, figs, and such, and offal, that others may not regard as food.

Nor is it a job for the greedy, since you must try to conceal your intervention, and eat the bare minimum of each item.

The Boss does not want to look at his plate and see bits gone astray, and observe that someone else has enjoyed the best part of his meal before him.

The Boss likes food but the food is not always kind to him. His dentures are ill-fitting and can chafe his gums. He expects to be warned when hard chewing is required.

He hates being surprised by piping hot or chilled foods, which put his remaining teeth on edge.

The Boss will usually trust a bottle with the seals intact, uncorked or with the screw-top unbroken. Anything opened must first be sampled by the taster.

It is easy to tamper with cigars and cigarettes, so opened packets have to be sampled, before the Boss can inhale with confidence.

So, in fulfilling the demands of the job I become, at only twelve years of age, both a light smoker and a heavyish drinker.

* * *

I am not a snitch or a tell-tale. I would never rat on another person. Not on purpose.

So I never mean to get Professor Nikolai

Anichkov, President of the Academy of Medical Sciences, into trouble. I don't even know him. It comes about quite by accident. It happens this way.

Matryona comes to find me in the rehearsal room in the afternoon. She says the Boss has called for me to taste his breakfast.

The Sick-Man is cheerful, and smiles to see me. But he complains about his rheumatism, cranky heart and creaking bones, and says to me —

'It is an evil thing getting old. The head is willing, but the body won't oblige.'

Naturally, I say, 'Then you should get yourself an *auto-jektor*.'

To be quite honest, I didn't mean it seriously. I meant it as a joke.

'What?' he frowns. Because — I've learned — he does not welcome other people knowing things he does not know. Himself.

I explain it as best I can. An *autojektor* is the heart-and-lung machine used by Professor Sergei Brukhonenko to keep alive the head of a dog, after he has severed it from its body. Papa has told me all about it. I assumed the Sick-Man knew all about it too. After all, he paid for it.

I thought everyone had seen those pictures of the live head of a dog, looking none too happy, separate from its body, joined to a relay of tubes, lying on an enamelled tray, growling and snarling at a circle of scientists.

'So you could keep your head alive,' I explain, 'on a plate, and not have to bother about your sick old body.'

'But this is *immortality* for *the mind*,' the Sick-Man says. 'Why has nobody told me any of this?'

'Or, if you prefer,' I suggest, 'you could get a newer, younger body.'

'How,' the Sick-Man demands, 'do I get another body?'

He sounds really interested now. I can see from the perfect stillness of his unblinking eyes that I have his full attention.

'Well,' I say, 'it's not straightforward, but Professor Vladimir Demikhov did it with a dog.'

'Did what?'

'He grafted a second head onto a dog's body. So I'm sure they can do the same with people.'

'He put an old head on a new body?' he asks. 'Truly?'

'Yes,' I say, 'but . . .'

I mention some of the drawbacks. Obvious really. You'd have to share the same body with someone else. That is, the head already on there. The current tenant. Naturally, there's a loss of privacy.

Then, you'd have two heads, which must single you out socially, and draw attention, especially — for instance — at public events, like the annual May Day Parade in Victory Square.

Then there might well be disagreements. The two heads might be in two different minds about things — about what to do with your parts, and who was in charge of what . . . But you'd have the use of a newer, healthier body.

'Yes?'

'And the newer, healthier body would get the advantage of your experience of life. It could be a good deal all round.'

But for some reason, I have made the Sick-Man very angry. His face is flushed crimson. There's a twitch to his cheeks. His nostrils are flared.

He has picked up the receiver of the green Bakelite telephone. He is shouting into the mouthpiece.

'Get me the President of the Academy of Medical Sciences . . . '

I hear a distant squeaking sound from the other end of the line.

'Yes, *Nikolai Anichkov,*' he mutters. 'Have him here, within the hour . . . '

The Boss shakes his head in angry disbelief.

'Traitors,' he growls.

'Yes?' say I.

'For years I support research into fighting old age. Now immortality is made possible, through Socialist science. And I'm the last to know . . . Do they *not* want me to live forever?'

The sadness cuts me to the bone. So I'm struggling to remember the word for it *when-you-are-incredibly-powerful-and-yet-fatally-weak-because-you-still-remain-human.*

You may be the most powerful man in the world but still you can't dodge death. When you have to go, you have to go.

7

The Juggler's Life

'I guess that's a fine career,' I say to Felix, 'being a double for Comrade Iron-Man. Every bit as good as being his personal Food-Taster, Technician First Class.'

Felix ponders this without expression or reply. He examines the shiny toes of his boots. He brushes some lint from the sleeve of his Marshal's jacket.

I can tell he is dejected from the day's *How-To-Behave-Like-Comrade-Iron-Man* Lessons with Director Dikoy. There was a deal of shouting, complaint and criticism. But not a lot of progress was made. The Director was harsh, with exacting standards that Felix never came close to meeting. So I do my best to cheer him up.

'You must get to travel,' I suggest. 'You meet important people. Everyone pays you respect.'

'It is a job for life,' says Felix. 'But you can never be sure how long that life will be . . . '

'You do a service for the Motherland, and for the Party, and for Comrade Iron-Man himself,' I say.

'It is well worth the sacrifices,' says Felix, looking over his shoulder to check there is no one in earshot.

'Sacrifices?' I ask.

'Well, you see . . . ' Felix sighs, 'the way it is . . . '

★   ★   ★

The way Felix tells it, he was at heart a happy, warm-spirited man, who enjoyed all life had to offer. He liked to walk on the sunny side of the street, and bask on the bright side. He made sure his glass was always half-full, and never half-empty.

He trained at circus school as a juggler and dancer. He joined a theatre troupe in Yekaterinburg. He liked best working at the Puppet Theatre, or the Theatre of Musical Komedy, or doing private parties for the children of Party officials.

He liked to wear grease-paint, or masks, or animal costumes that completely covered his head and concealed his true appearance. Because, when he was made-up or dressed up, he looked different. People no longer saw any unfortunate resemblances in his face.

But suppose he went out without make-up, and in normal attire, into a loud, crowded tavern, or a busy restaurant, or the wedding reception for a cousin, or a school reunion, or the terrace at a football ground, the same things always happened, as night follows day.

The gathering would fall silent. People would melt away from his side. The world looked at him sideways, while pretending he just wasn't there. There's an elephant in the room. They think their pretence not to see it will make it disappear.

He hears the whispers and muttering.

'It can't be!'

'But look at him.'

'That face.'

Because, even without a moustache, and despite his youth, he bears an extraordinary, uncanny likeness to Comrade Iron-Man, General Secretary of the Central Committee of the Communist Party of the Socialist Union.

Sometimes, your face tells fibs about you. So, although he is a kindly, comradely soul, he seems to wear an attitude of haughty disdain.

Most people realise he is probably not Marshal Iron-Man. But they remain uneasy. Is the Party checking up on them? Is it some elaborate ploy to test their loyalty? Is he some close relative — son or brother maybe — who has the ear, or shares the authority, of the Great Leader?

Then, when the Germans invade, Felix signs up to defend the Motherland. Now he can just be a normal guy. A private soldier in infantry uniform, like any other, he thinks. But no.

The officers pass him from unit to unit. No one wants him in their Company. He is, at best, an embarrassment. Perhaps, at worst, a terrible omen. A death sentence, maybe.

'Private Dadaev,' he salutes the Captain, 'reporting for service. Ready to fight in the defence of the Glorious Motherland.'

'Yes?' The Captain frowns, winces, and shakes the private's hand with a very timid deference. 'It is a privilege to meet your honour.'

'Where do I report, sir?'

'I would not like to say,' says the Commander. 'I would not like to order you to do anything or report anywhere. It is entirely up to you, Comrade. Please please yourself. But please please yourself somewhere else, if you prefer.'

'If it pleases *you*,' says Felix, 'I would like to fight the Nazi scum, and die a heroic death, here, in defence of Mother Motherland.'

The Sergeant whispers to the Lieutenant, who speaks in the ear of the Captain.

'Somewhere else would be better . . . ' he tells Felix. 'Regrettably, it is not permissible for you to die here, with us. You must take your ultimate sacrifice elsewhere. This is a travel warrant. Collect some extra rations. You must take yourself to Kursk and join the 95th Rifle Division. They are in much greater need of your heroic death over there.'

So he is passed from pillar to post. In the end, he takes matters into his own hands. He jumps into a trench with the 192nd Infantry Division of the 12th Army at the defence of Uman and gets himself killed, almost, in his first half-hour's engagement, when he peeps over the rim of the trench and is shot through the neck by a German sniper.

As he lies dying, the life's blood squirting out of his neck, pumping in a jerky arc, he hears the medics talk about him.

'Such a perfect likeness.'

'Have you told the Political Commissar?'

★   ★   ★

When Felix next wakes, it is many days later, in a cool white-tiled room that smells of Lysol. And, alas, is not Heaven.

He feels a terrible burning to both his cheeks. He has been given some extra operations, after they resuscitated him and stitched up the holes where the bullet passed through. He has had his ears re-shaped. And they have burned some livid pits on his cheeks with hydrochloric acid, to resemble Comrade Iron-Man's smallpox scars.

He is in some secret medical unit just outside The Kapital, in the hands of the People's Commissariat for Internal Affairs. It is not a happy awakening.

They tell him he is dead. Dead every which way.

Dead to his family, who have been informed of his demise and shown his grave.

Dead to his old name and identity, now he has no papers.

Dead to his old career as an entertainer.

Dead to his former face. Now he is the spit of Comrade Iron-Man.

★ ★ ★

'At least I didn't have a wife and children,' says Felix.

'What difference would that make?' I ask.

'When you become a double, everyone *disappears* in time. All your close family . . . '

'Disappears?' I ask.

'They are wiped, erased, off the face of the world. So no one is alive who can recognise you any more,' Felix says, 'and know you by your old name. And say you are not really Iron-Man.'

'Oh.'

'You lose your name, and your family and friends, your past and your future . . . ' says Felix. 'But, apart from that, and apart from when you get shot at by some foreign assassins, being a double for Comrade Iron-Man is, as you remark, a fine career with great prospects . . . '

★ ★ ★

Yesterday, the Boss tells me a true story. He likes telling jokes about his very best friends and closest colleagues, who often turn out to be his favourite enemies.

Comrade Krushka goes to visit a collective pig farm. They say he has a very jolly, friendly temperament, when he is not in a mammoth rage, or purging peasants in the Borderlands. He clambers into a pig pen and pats the pigs who gather round him, sniffing, snuffling and snorting, welcoming a kindred spirit into their gang.

Next day, *The Daily Truth* publishes a photo of the happy scene. Beneath the picture is the caption: *A group of pigs greet Comrade Krushka (third from left).*

So when the plump, round-faced, hairless, pink person, with a wobbly under-chin, and droopy dewlaps, waddles up to me smiling from pointy ear to pointy ear, I guess immediately who he is. It has to be the porker Krushka.

'Are you the boy who plays draughts with the Boss?'

'That's me,' I agree. 'My name is Yuri.'

'You are fortunate, Yuri. The Boss has taken a shine to you. They say he confides private, personal things to you. Do you know why?'

I shrug.

'You are right,' he says. 'It's hard to know why the Boss likes someone. But hates his identical twin. In your case, he may like you because you are a child, a fool and harmless. And you have a kind way, and an angel's face . . . '

'He says I'm a *perfect* fool,' I explain. 'He says he has several absolute idiots working for him, but I am his favourite.'

'That may be the answer,' he nods. 'But sometimes the Boss likes someone, and likes them some more, and then likes them even more than that. And then guess what happens next . . . '

'No idea.'

'It turns out they were a traitor. All along. Taking advantage of the Boss's trusting nature. So then they get arrested. And shot.'

'Really?'

'True. And guess what happens after that?'

'No idea.'

'They are nowhere to be seen. They are disappeared. Completely. And not just themselves. But their family too. They are disinvented. Evaporated. Annulled. Cancelled. Erased. Entirely. Not just their present, nor their future. Their past is gone too. Their face has fled from every photograph. Now, there's just an empty space, to the right of the Boss, where they used to appear. They evaporate from people's memory. Their name disappears from the index of books. In the Slavic Encyclopaedia, some writer has to fill out an extra three pages on the Kamenovska Tapeworm, after Lev Kamenev gets shot, just to fill the empty space.'

'Lev Kamenev?' I say. 'Who's he?'

'Yes . . . ' Krushka nods. 'My point exactly. Who indeed? Nobody knows any more. And do you know the moral of the story?'

'No.'

'Never, never underestimate the Boss. And never, never betray him.'

'Understood.'

'As it happens, there's a little task you can do. You'll never guess what it is.'

'Is it to keep my eyes and ears open, and report back to you?'

'Well said . . . ' He blinks and frowns his surprise. 'How on earth did you know?'

I shrug. 'I'm new to politics,' I admit, 'but I'm picking it up . . . '

'Now, we are true and good friends, you and I,' he declares. 'We shall never be parted. We shall never fall out. You must call me *Uncle Nikita*. I am not a bad man, you know.'

'No?'

'But, for the moment, it is messy.' He wrinkles his piggy nose at his misfortune.

'Messy?'

'Alas, I am up to my elbows in blood.'

I guess this is his colourful way of saying he has done some things he regrets.

'So many bullets. So many lists. So many pits to be dug. So much quicklime. It's Hell itself to organise.'

'Yes?'

'When you live with wolves, you must act like a wolf . . . *Owww* . . . *Oww* . . . ' He sticks out a pink tongue, looks upwards, as if addressing the moon, then commences to howl like a lonely wolf. It is not a good, realistic impression. Maybe he intends it just as a joke.

'Yes?'

'Yet, in my heart I am kind. My dog loves me. He worships the ground I walk upon. He is a Finnish Spitz called Tommi. I do not scare my children. Except when I mean to. My wife respects me. To my family I am gentle.'

'Good,' I say.

'Some people cannot separate their work and their family.'

'Yes?'

'I knew a prosecutor in Leninstadt who would go home every night and interrogate his loved ones — often with electricity.'

'Oh?'

'Some can't switch off, you see. They go home and arrest their relatives. I mention no names. Or throw their friends into prison. Or report their mother to the Secret Police. Or put their wife in a work camp. Before they know what's hit them, they are kissing the lift attendant at work, and sleeping with their stenographer, and married to their job.'

'Really?'

'It is not that way with me.'

'Good.'

'No executions in my cellars,' he smiles. 'No show-trials in the bedroom,' he grins. 'No work camps in the kitchen.'

Then he lifts me off the ground, hugs the breath from me and plants a damp, hot, onion-and-spittle kiss on my forehead.

'Together we will look after the Boss,' he says, 'now he is sickly, in his hour of need . . . We both know. His head is not right. So keep a close eye on Malarkov and Bruhah . . . Listen out. Tell me, if you hear anything odd. Or if they get up to anything *suspicious* . . . '

★ ★ ★

When Marshal Bruhah passes me in the corridor later that day, he hands me a small white envelope.

'Here,' he says, 'I have a message from your father . . . '

'Thank you, sir. Where is Papa?'

Bruhah holds a finger to his lips. 'Shhh,' he says, 'Read.'

True enough, it is a note from Papa, but his writing looks large and shaky —

My Very Dearest Son Yuri

This is to let you know I am well and healthy.

Marshal Bruhah has me in his protection. He is a good, kind man who cares for our welfare.

Do whatever he asks of you, to the letter, and without hesitation, however strange his requests may seem.

Then everything may end happily.

Your ever loving Papa

'Where can I find him?' I ask. Something makes me feel uneasy.

'Shhh.' Bruhah looks around in alarm. 'Walls have ears. It is a secret. But he is safe. He is nearby. He asked me to look after you.'

'Yes?' I say. 'It's just the note has no date.'

I think the Marshal senses my doubts, for

he reaches into his jacket pocket and removes an object wrapped in a white, red-speckled handkerchief. He lays it on his open palm, and uncovers it.

'There!' he says. 'Do you recognise these?'

'Why, yes,' I say, 'they are Papa's dentures.'

'He asked me to show you.'

'Why?'

'As proof he is well, and with me.'

'What's that?' I ask. There's a liver-coloured glob stuck to the back molar, and a crimson smear.

'Just a small piece of food,' says Bruhah. 'Or maybe he has a mouth ulcer.'

'But how can he eat, without his dentures?'

'Good point,' Bruhah nods wisely. 'I am going back to The Kapital shortly. I will return them to him immediately. So he can enjoy his supper.'

What can I do? I cannot call the Minister for Internal Security a liar. We are in his power, Papa and I.

But I feel most uneasy.

Papa is a very private, careful man. It is not like him to part from his dentures, or send them on errands ahead of him, in someone else's pocket.

8

Bringing Up Baby

The Boss likes to watch a film late every night with his close colleagues, and choicest enemies, before they all take dinner together.

Because he has been unwell, with high blood pressure, and does not care to travel, they show the movie on a portable projector in the large dining room here in the dacha, with the audience lounging on sofas, rather than at his personal kinema in the Palace of the People.

His projectionist, Ivan Sanchin, has come over, together with the Minister for Kinema, Ivan Bolshakov, to organise this entertainment.

'Tell me, Comrade Minister,' the Boss asks, smiling grim, with more teeth than warmth, like a krocodile, 'what film do you have for our viewing tonight?'

The Minister is nervous to address the lofty sections of the Politburo. He wears a pinstripe suit, and has a starched collar that swallows his neck. His forehead glistens pink. Beads of sweat are descending his cheeks. He clears his throat, then coughs. 'Tonight I have *Yankee* film . . . '

The collected Ministers hiss and boo. But this is just a mean sham — a pretence of loyalty to Slavic Film Making, because I already hear Deputy Malarkov whisper to Comrade Bulgirov —

'Please let it be some Hollywood movie with busts and legs and swimsuits . . . not some home-grown bollocks about collective farming, or some Bulgarian cartoon shit about fairies . . . '

Anyway, everyone knows the Boss enjoys USA movies, especially Cowboy and Indian slaughters, Gangsters betraying each other, and shooting each other dead, especially James Cagney, and the Tarzan series about this wild man, and his animal friends in the jungle.

Minister Bolshakov coughs again nervously, then raises his shaky hand to calm the gathering. Beneath his arm, his jacket is darkened with a giant circle of sweat.

'With great respect,' he says, 'this is film by distinguished director Comrade Howard Hawks, famous for gangster movie *Scarface*, cowboy film *The Outlaw* and detective movie *The Big Sleep*. But this movie is different. It is film about culture of Amerikan Life. It is called *Bringing Up Baby*.'

'A documentary? About child-care?' The

117

Boss sounds peeved. He looks grim.

'Not child-care. Not documentary,' says Bolshakov, 'but crazy, laugh-a-minute, wet-your-pants, *screwball* komedy. Showing the decadence and futility of Amerikan Life.'

They say the poor Minister has to spend his whole day learning about a movie before showing it to the Chairman. To make sure there are no naked-lady-parts, anti-Communistic propaganda, or rude appearances by the insufferable face of John Wayne.

'Roll it, then,' says the Boss, 'and let's hope it's funny. And there's no nudity. Because we are not running a brothel here . . . And Bolshakov, is the dialogue in English?'

'Yes, Comrade Chairman.'

'Then you'd better translate as we go along . . . '

Bolshakov coughs.

'This is Palaeontologist. He has assembled an entire brontosaurus skeleton . . .

'It is missing only one bone to make it complete . . .

'The intercostal clavicle . . .

'Now we see the same man, later this day. Now he is playing golfs . . .

'Golfs is a popular, petit-bourgeois find-the-hole, ball-and-stick leisure-game . . .

'You must push the white ball into the small tunnel . . .

'The man who makes the fewest pokes is the winner . . . '

Lucky day for Bolshakov. He takes longer and longer pauses. He starts to trust the film to talk for itself.

It is funny. Man and woman argue. Woman steals man's golfs ball. Woman drives car into man's car.

Soon most Ministers have laughed, one or more times. Out loud. Even the Boss has been seen to chuckle.

And most of the action is obvious, so you don't need so much translation. Handsome man meets beautiful woman. Then they argue forever. Until, in the end, they get married. Then they can argue for life.

At first, the film presents a strong impression of life in the USA. It is sunny all day. There is no work. People are good-looking. Everyone has their own car, even women. Shops are full of foods and products. Meals are taken in expensive, glamorous restaurants. Men wear only suits. Women wear only fashionable dresses, and clank their jewellery.

But there are many small, Kapitalist, bourgeois mishaps along the way including two car crashes. Woman tears man's jacket. Man tears woman's dress, exposing her undergarments and bottom. When woman

119

falls into a pond, the wet clothes stick tight to her body, particularly round the bumps and into the curves.

Bruhah applauds. Krushka whistles through his fingers.

Pet dog buries valuable, missing dinosaur bone. Woman has tame leopard as pet. It likes listening to music, in particular the popular song 'I Can't Give You Anything But Love, Baby', but it gets exchanged with wild leopard that growls, bites and takes no interest in vernacular music.

This can happen because you take your leopard for a drive in the back seat of your motor car and it swaps places with an identical leopard escaped from a travelling circus, just passing through town.

I believe, for convenience, they get the same cat (of species *Panthera pardus*) with unchanged spots to play both leopards. They say he is very same well-connected, highly regarded cat actor that stars in the *Tarzan* movies.

At the end, the Boss stops chuckling, the lights go back on, and he gives a short speech.

He says that Bolshakov has chosen a very bad film for us to watch, but that he is forgiven because it is an educational, good-bad film that demonstrates the decadence of the West, and the parasitical life of the Amerikan rich.

In this film, he says, you don't see a single person do a single job of work.

He says there is another strange thing. There are thirteen million black people in Amerika. But none in this movie.

'Bolshakov . . . ' he barks, 'who is this leading male actor?'

'That is *Cary Grant.*'

'Anyone notice anything remarkable and striking about this Cary Grant?' the Boss enquires.

There is a long silence. No one wants to chance a wrong answer.

'Here . . . ' says the Boss. 'I give you a clue . . . ' He swivels sideways, to display his profile.

The painful silence continues. But I've guessed the solution.

'Excuse the faulty opinions of a child without political insight, and with traumatic damage to the Frontal Lobes of his cortex . . . ' I pipe up, 'but doesn't this Cary Grant look a lot like you?'

There is sudden murmuring of muffled agreement.

'Exactly,' says the Boss. 'He looks like me. But not so much like me as that other actor . . . ' He pauses to summon the name of his look-alike from the tip of his tongue.

'*Clark Gable,*' Bolshakov volunteers.

'Exactly,' the Boss clarifies the confusion, 'Cary Grant does not resemble me so much as Clark Gable resembles me . . . in that film . . . '

'*It Happened One Night*,' Bolshakov announces.

'Exactly,' says the Boss. 'In the kinematographically significant, culturally memorable, anthropologically important, politically enlightening film *It Happened One Night*, Clark Gable has a moustache and smokes a pipe. People have remarked it is hard to tell him apart from Chairman Iron-Man.'

There is applause. For the film, for the Boss's observations, for his similarity to Clark Gable.

And on that happy note, the company takes itself to supper in the large dining room.

I think of Papa. And I trust he is reunited with his teeth. So he too can enjoy a good supper.

★   ★   ★

Now comes the time for me to work. But no one tells me to stay. No one tells me where to go. No one notices I'm even there.

I'm the invisible taster. Standing between the Boss and poison, the General Secretary and Death.

122

There is a long table down the middle of the room, laid with a white cloth, candlesticks, china plates, crystal glasses and fancy cutlery.

The side table is stacked with steaming salvers, platters of fish, joints of meat, baskets of breads, boards of cheese, bowls of cooked vegetables.

First off, to break the ice, the gathering plays a game of *guess-the-temperature*. The Boss holds a mercury thermometer. And everyone must give their estimate.

Krushka guesses wrong by six degrees centigrade and has to drink six glasses of vodka. Bruhah is out by two and has to down a couple of glasses.

Bulgirov gets the temperature exactly right. And, as a punishment for acting superior and being too clever by half, he is made to drink seven glasses, then to crawl all round the dinner table, on his hands and knees, braying like a donkey.

Then they take the soup course. There is borscht or a wild mushroom pottage. The Boss takes a bowl of each, then pours one into the other, to mix them, then crumbles in some bread, to thicken the mix, then spoons it avidly into his mouth.

I take first sip. I cannot claim it is a happy marriage. The purple spiciness and the mushroom earthiness are not a good mix and don't taste like friends.

For a small man, he has a large presence and a big appetite.

There is Georgian wine to drink, which the Boss calls *fruit juice* because it is not so strong as some other wines, so you can drink whole bottles of it, to wash down the vodka, before getting slurred and falling over.

After the soup there is folk dancing. The Boss selects someone who must then dance around the table for the others. Malarkov is chosen to do the Troika, which means he must jump high in the air and, with his arms outstretched, put the soles of his feet together, so his limbs form a diamond. Ideally he must hover in mid-air, a metre above the ground.

But because he is fat and over seventy, and breathes very heavily while sweating a lot, and is crimson-faced, and cannot launch his feet more than five centimetres off the ground, his attempt does not present itself as athletic or graceful.

So, the Boss observes, 'Sit down, you're a disgrace, you tub of lard,' and instead gets Krushka to dance the Kalinka.

And I have to say that for a big, heavy man, he swivels delicately with his hands on his hips, and wiggles his ample wobbly bottom, does mincing, backward steps with great precision, and swirls like a ballerina, and everyone whistles and claps in time, so the Boss lets him carry on for ten minutes, or more, till the sweat is rolling down his crimson face in rivulets, till you see the Deputy's eyes pleading to be allowed to stop. But, as Comrade Krushka told me earlier, when the Boss says 'Jump', you ask 'How high?'

Then there is great hilarity because Malarkov, who is wearing a spotless white naval suit, has sat down on several over-ripe tomatoes that some villain has placed on his chair, so he now sports a damp red bottom, like a baboon in heat.

So the Boss insists Malarkov takes off his trousers so a member of the household staff can take them away and clean them. But you can see from his face and manner that Malarkov was much happier as he was before, wearing trousers like everyone else, without exposing his underwear and naked knees and shin-garters holding up his sulphur-yellow socks.

Then they take the fish course. There are pickled herrings, pike baked in a salt crust, and grilled perch with a green-herb sauce.

A lot of wine and vodka has been drunk. The talk is loud, but their speech not as clear as before, now everyone's tongue has loosened.

It's then that the Boss tells an interesting story how he ran twenty kilometres through the snow as a child in bare feet, before swimming across a freezing lake, then shooting twelve mallards with his catapult. Truly, the Kind Uncle is the Man of Iron.

Then everyone applauds. Then guests get their chance to sing a song for the others.

Malarkov sings 'Smuglianka — Death to Fascism, Freedom to the People'. Bulgirov gives us 'Cossacks Never Say Die', while Krushka sings a peace-time song, with lively hand and tongue gestures, called 'Olga's Tits'.

★   ★   ★

Comrade Dikoy has been watching from the corner of the table. He appears tonight not as a double for the General Secretary but as guest, actor and celebrity. It is rumoured that the Iron-Man is a great admirer of his work and will have no one else take his part in films.

But now the leading double appears without a Marshal's uniform, and shorn of his stage-moustache, and paste-on sideburns, with his lank, curly hair flopping over his brow, rather than combed back over his crown, and wearing a leather jacket and a beret. He has a more bohemian look and barely resembles the Great Father now.

Although he hasn't touched any food, he has a large array of glasses in front of him, and frequently refills his tumbler with vodka, which he then dilutes with German schnapps.

His eyes are piercing embers. His voice is slurred.

'Look at them . . . ' he leans over and whispers, his boozy breath hot into my ear. 'The leaders of the Socialist World.' He points to them in turn. 'The one who murdered the peasants . . . The one who murdered the Revolution . . . The one who murdered all his friends and family . . . And the one who picks women off the street, fucks them, strangles them, then buries them in his garden.'

'Really?' I say. 'Which?' I didn't know.

'Suppose you got all the most ambitious and ruthless men in the nation, and locked them in a room together, and called it, say, *the Communist Party Congress of 1945*, and left them alone to quietly, calmly murder each other . . . '

'Yes?'

'That's who you have left, when all the head-butting, kicking, eye-gouging, cannibalism, ear-chewing and back-stabbings have reduced their number to five . . . '

'Oh . . . ' I say.

'So,' he asks, 'who will be next?'

'Next?'

'For the chop . . . '

'I don't understand.'

'We have a lion, a tiger, a bear, a python and an alligator. All in the same cage. I think there will be fatalities. In the end, only one can be left alive . . . It is no secret . . . They all know this . . . '

'Yes?' I ask. It's news to me.

'Who will win? Who scares you the most?'

'It's hard . . . ' I hesitate, 'I don't know them well enough, but . . . '

'Yes?'

'Bruhah broke my nose. I'm sure he did it on purpose.'

'Good choice.' He slaps my back. 'Well chosen . . . The rest are all evil bastards, but even they are scared of Bruhah . . . Even Bruhah is scared of Bruhah . . . Bruhah is the beast of beasts. He is the monsters' monster . . . But, because he is the worst, the others might gang together to eliminate him first . . . '

'Is it quite safe, Comrade,' I ask, 'to talk this way?' I admire Director Dikoy. I don't want his friendship with the bottle to get him into trouble. I gesture to the Magnates, at the senior end of the table. 'Someone might overhear . . . '

'Who knows . . . ' he slurs. He splays his palms. 'Is it safe to be human?'

I shrug.

'Is it safe to think? Is it safe to care? Is it safe to breathe?'

Then the shutters come down on his eyes. He promptly topples sideways, off his chair, and sprawls still on the ground. I think he's passed out. He seems to be kissing the floor. Now gravity has had its way with him, he seems to have no upright plans of his own.

★   ★   ★

Myself, I am feeling light-headed too, because I've been not only sampling the different courses of food, but sipping the variety of liquor and beverages including Hungarian hock, Czechoslovakian cherry beer, Hungarian Bulls Blood wine, German lager, peach nectar, Polish vodka, Scottish whisky, French absinthe, Estonian brandy, Finnish cloudberry liqueur and Slovenian schnapps.

All the small sips add up. It is a lot for a twelve-year-old to take in, new to alcohol.

I step out swaying on my feet, and trip downstairs to the visitors' toilets and find

Minister Bulgirov there ahead of me, perched on a marble toilet in a cubicle, with the door wide open.

His eyes are closed. His head has swayed to the side. His arms hang limp at his sides. His open palms are splayed towards me. His trousers lie crumpled round his ankles.

Naturally, you worry. Even the youngest of these Ministers are getting on, and stretching their lease on life.

'First Deputy?' I tap his shoulder. 'Are you well?' By which I really mean, 'Are you *dead*?'

His glazed eyes flicker. He blinks and takes me in.

'Piss-heads . . . ' he says. 'All they do is drink, drink, drink.'

'Are you unwell?' I ask.

'Tired unto death,' he groans, 'and drunk as a sailor. This is the only sleep I get.'

'Oh.'

'Will you do me a favour, kid?'

'Ask,' I say, 'and it's yours.'

'Let me sleep. Let me sleep the just sleep of the dead,' he says. 'Give me seven sublime, whole, complete, entire, uninterrupted minutes. Then wake me up . . . '

'Is seven enough?'

'Usually, kid, I have to make do with five or six.'

And, sure enough, when I wake him, after

watching the slow passing of time on the mother-of-pearl inlaid face of his jewelled, gold Rolex wristwatch, with the krocodile-leather strap, he seems alert, jolly and much refreshed.

'Good kid,' he beams, brushing some dust from the lapel of his jacket. 'That was a great catnap. I'm in your debt. Come,' he says, 'let's get back, and have a drink. We're missing all the entertainment.'

True enough. Upstairs, when we rejoin the company, there's fun all round. Through the dining room window we can see that the Deputy Minister for Foreign Affairs is trying to grapple the Yugoslav Ambassador into the duck pond, while inside, at the long table, we find that the Boss is arm-wrestling the dacha guards, and beating everyone with devastating ease, including Sergeant Igor Stavrov, weight-lifting champion of the entire Slav Army.

The Kind Uncle, the Great Father, is not called the Man of Iron for nothing.

9

The Sunlight in the Garden

Next morning, after breakfast, the Boss invites me to walk with him in the garden.

'Follow me, boy,' he says. 'Don't scuff your feet. And stop sniffing. And don't speak unless you are spoken to. I don't need your endless prattle. I want to enjoy the birdsong.'

He strides in front, and addresses his remarks to the space behind, as I trudge in his wake.

It is the end of February. There is a thin scatter of snow on the grass and treacherous grey slush on the path.

I realise it is the first time I have been out of the dacha, and in the open air and sunlight, since we first arrived.

I smell pine, earth and manure. Gone are the scents of wood panelling, floor polish and simmering cabbage. The cold air prickles on my cheeks and stings in my nostrils. I feel a tingle to my ears. The Boss spouts misty gusts of breath as he talks.

'Do you know the best flower?' he asks.

'Well . . . ' I say, 'the camomile gives us

medicine. And the crocus is very beautiful.'

'Perhaps,' he concedes. 'But the very best flower is the mimosa. It brings us hope. It raises the human spirit because it heralds the spring, and the end of our long, cold suffering.'

Then the Boss looks upward and pauses, swivelling round to face me. I watch him as he closes his eyes in recollection and begins to recite —

> The bud has opened; now the rose
> brushes the tender violet.
> The lily, leant above the grass
> By grazing breezes, slumbers not.
>
> The lark, chirping its warbling tune,
> Skims high between the clouds;
> Meanwhile, the nightingale sounds
> Its sweet, mellifluous serenade:
>
> 'Break forth in blossom Slavic land!
> As shivers of joy within you spread.
> While you must study, tiny friend,
> To delight your Motherland!'

'That's beautiful,' I say. 'Is it a song? Or a poem?'

'A poem.'

'Who wrote it? Pushkin?'

'I wrote it myself,' says the Boss. 'It is called 'Morning'. I wrote it when I was young and a romantic, before the Revolution, even.'

'Do you still write poetry?'

The Boss frowns and worries the gravel, chivvying the stones with the toe of his left boot.

'When I was a young man, I thought it was enough to write my poetry in words. But now I make my poetry out of people.'

'You do?'

'Gaiety is the great feature of our national life. I write joy and hope. I inscribe it in the lives of the people.'

'That's nice,' I agree.

'Also, I deliver the law. Which is the poetry of power, and the rhythm of duty, and the rhyme of order.'

'Yes?'

'We will visit the roses,' says the Boss. 'We will see how they have withstood the winter cold. There is a secret to tending roses. Can you guess what it is?'

'You must feed and water them well? And always treat them with kindness.'

'Not that. Far from it. They must learn to be tough and fend for themselves. The secret is to be stern with them. You must love them, but you must love them harshly.'

The Boss swings open the door to the long,

low hut. There are three parallel flower beds running the length of the wooden-framed, glass building.

There are lines of spiky, black-stemmed, leafless, bloomless bushes, apparently dead. The base of each is locked in a cone of compacted earth.

'The secret with roses is to cut them back. Their beauty only comes from a harsh, pitiless discipline.'

'It does?'

'You must cut out all the unhealthy or diseased tissue. You must *dead-head* the blooms that have lost their vigour and beauty. Do you know what the growing parts of the stems are called?'

'No?'

'They are called *the leaders*. If you do not cut the leaders back by a half, at least, the plants grow too fast, without strength or discipline. Then they will bear stunted blooms.'

★ ★ ★

A food-taster may not get much sleep. Not if he works for Comrade Iron-Man, Kind Uncle, Great Father. He can be kept up until four or five in the morning.

'I'm an insomniac, Yuri. I do not sleep well.

135

I feel tired most of the time. All the while my younger colleagues try to outsmart me with their energetic, fresh minds. But I cannot have them alert and sober, trying to run rings around me . . . '

'No?'

'So, I make sure they get no more sleep than me. And that they drink too much. It is a brake on their enthusiasm. It deadens their minds.'

'Yes?'

'It is no more than common sense. I make them come here every night for supper. And I do not let them go until they are drunk and I, myself, am tired enough to sleep. Then, in the morning, I may ring them early to make sure they are awake, at work at their desks.'

★   ★   ★

The late hours exhaust the Magnates. They tire me too.

I'd taken to snoozing, fully clothed, on blankets behind a sofa in the small dining room. Then I could manifest immediately, from nowhere, when summoned to my tasting duties.

This morning I wake to an exchange of gruff male voices. It is Bruhah and Krushka on either side of the dining table, leaning forward so their heads nearly touch, as if ready to butt each other like stags. They are eyeballing each other steadily, each challenging the other to look down or away.

I guess they think they're alone, because they're talking softly, but with menace, with the doors closed. So, I'm slow to show my face.

'If he throws hedgehogs under me,' observes Krushka, 'I'll throw porcupines under him.'

'He's gunning for Myokan and Motolov,' says Bruhah. 'He wants their heads.'

'Yes,' Krushka nods, 'but for a mad dog, seven versts is just a short detour.'

'He's coming after me,' says Bruhah, 'I know it. He's constructing a case. He's fabricating evidence. He's getting people to sign papers.'

'Yes, your elbow is close,' says Krushka, 'but you still can't bite it.'

'He wants to eliminate the doctors. He wants to put all the Jews into camps. And there are new orders out to assassinate Tito. He's planning to take on Amerika,' says Bruhah. 'He thinks they'll attack us. So he wants to strike first.'

'It shows the goose can't be friends with the pig,' says Krushka. 'He sees only enemies. He knows only threats.'

'Yes . . . ' says Bruhah. 'No doubt.'

'He'll have his hands full, if he tries to milk the bull.' Krushka makes a rude-looking gesture with his hand.

'Indeed?'

'So make the butter soon. Before the milk sours.'

'An act of finality . . . that can't be undone.'

'Now,' says Krushka. 'Quick. Get in there. While the milkmaid's still willing.'

'A natural event — a final stroke.'

It's then I decide to show myself. While they are still on the farming-talk. Before anything I shouldn't hear gets said, to get me into trouble.

'Don't mind me, kind Comrades,' I say, stepping out from behind the sofa. 'I'm just getting up. Is it morning already?'

They are most surprised to see me. As if I am some scary apparition. Bruhah jumps backward. Poor, pink Krushka goes white as a noodle.

'Were you listening?' says Krushka.

'Why? Were you talking?' I say.

'What did you hear?' asks Bruhah.

'Why? Did you say something?' I ask.

'You're a fool, aren't you, Yuri?' Bruhah's glare melts to a sly smile.

'You're a moron, aren't you?' Krushka taps

me on the shoulder.

'I am.'

I was most surprised to see them hug each other and exchange kisses to both cheeks. Then whisper to each other while taking a backward glance to me.

I could only catch their last few words as they turn to gaze on me: ' . . . wait till it's done.'

★ ★ ★

I never knew that Bruhah and Krushka were so friendly, to meet together, and sort things out, like now, without the Boss to guide and advise them.

It was said Bruhah made himself unpleasant to the others by threatening to arrest their wives, and do rude, unkind things to them in prison. But you never knew if he really meant it. Because he'd had Motolov's wife Karolina imprisoned, so people said, but then kept her alive and hardly touched her.

And he'd stand too close to the other Magnates at the urinal, downstairs at the dacha, and peer sideways at their privates and smile.

And he'd slip over-ripe fruit into the pockets of Malarkov's white dress uniform, then pat his jacket from the outside to make the fruits burst, and spread broad, red, purple and orange circles over his uniform.

Or, he'd pop a special liquid into Terakov's wine glass, because it made you want to relieve yourself, but without warning, all of a sudden, in a hot lava flow, like a volcano.

But when Terakov worked out who did it, he had Bruhah's favourite Mercedes-Benz car crushed up to the size of a travel chest and left on his doorstep. Some people say the chauffeur is still at the wheel.

Bruhah and Malarkov would often share a limousine back to The Kapital, but never with either of the other two.

You'd sometimes find Krushka and Bulgirov whispering into each other's ears, in the same toilet compartment downstairs. But who knows what they were doing. Maybe they just liked to be close, like very firm chums.

It all reminded me of the lads at school, doing secret business in the lavatory at breaktime.

★   ★   ★

The Boss likes quoting the writer Chekhov —

When a person is born, he can embark on only one of three roads of life: if you go right, the wolves will eat you; if you go left, you'll eat

the wolves; if you go straight, you'll eat yourself.

But it always seemed gloomy. So alternatives keep coming to me.

'Can't you befriend the wolf? And tame him?' I ask, 'and make a pet dog of him? And maybe call him *Wolfie*?'

He says I am a fool and a romantic. He says I must have lived a safe life. He asks me about my home.

'Did your mother and father not beat you?' he asks. 'Viciously? Without reason? Like proper parents?'

'Never.'

'Never?' he scowls. 'Then how will you ever learn discipline? Doesn't your father get drunk, go crazy, and thrash you with a belt?'

'No, never.'

'Really?' He shakes his head. 'What kind of father is that? Then does your mother not hit you hard, for nothing, mornings and evenings, with a wooden spoon, or a broomstick, to teach you some respect?'

'No,' I say. 'Anyway, she can't. She's at a work camp at Kolyma.'

He nods. 'As I thought. She must be an anti-social element, then . . . or an enemy of the people.'

I shrug. I don't remember. I cannot say.

'Still, if you do not like your father,' the Boss advises, 'you can always get rid of him . . .'

'I can?'

'Report him to the Party. Say he is a reactionary. Say he is a Cosmopolitan spy. Say he listens to foreign radio. They will have him arrested. And sent to a camp. It will teach him a lesson. And you can be rid of him, for good.'

'But I love my father,' I say.

The Boss flares his nostrils as if sensing a bad smell, narrows his eyes and shakes his head. 'It can be good to respect your parents, up to a point, because it teaches you to love authority. But it is not proper to fall into sentimentality, and it's a crime to love your family more than you love Socialism, the Party or the Motherland.'

I shrug. I say I love all those more than my very own life but, in truth, this is not strictly so.

'People are weak,' he advises. 'People are not to be trusted. People cannot help themselves. In time, everyone betrays you . . . You want to be just but it's hard to forgive . . . When there's a person, there's a problem. When there's no person, there's no problem.'

'You don't trust anyone?'

'I trust no one.'

'Yourself?'

'Not even myself.'

I ask him if that is why he is not married. He tells me that his second wife shot herself. He says his first wife was called Kato and died of typhus, without a by-your-leave or warning . . .

'I loved people until Kato died. When she went, my last warm feelings for people passed away too.'

'Truly?' I say. 'You don't love people? That's strange.'

'The way it is.' The Boss is gruff, stiff and aggrieved. 'People have always let me down . . . '

'Yes?'

'I have taught myself to look people full in the face, in bright daylight, objectively, free from the glare of affection. Most human life is unnecessary. Futile. Tragic. Now, I see people for what they are — as transitory beasts in nature, as creatures passing from birth, through life to death. As Chekhov shows us, everything, everyone is in decay, rushing onwards to its decline and destruction . . .

'I see a person like this . . . ' He swats at a circling gnat. 'This fly was a maggot, then it was a larva. Next it will be a corpse, flat on its back with its feet in the air. It is born, it lives,

143

it buzzes around, it feeds on shit, it lays eggs, it dies. When I see a blizzard of flies swarming round a cow's arse, I do not think 'Aren't we lucky to live in such a golden, abundant age of flies? Thank goodness there's enough shit for them all. Why doesn't Comrade Shostakovich write a symphony to celebrate? Should we commission a heroic painting? Surely we should have more lyric poetry on this?'

'So, now, whenever I am considering a serious question, an issue of substance, concerning my fellow man, I substitute the words 'this fly' for the person's name. This helps me decide.

'It allows me to see objectively, free of false sentiment. So, I ask myself — 'Is this fly better than the next fly?', 'Will the world be a worse place if this fly dies?', ''Does this fly deserve the Lenin Prize, or should it go to the earwig instead?', 'Should I listen to this woodlouse, Eisenhower?', 'Is this bluebottle, with the shimmering chest, the most beautiful fly in the world?''

'Yes?' I say. 'You do?'

But I can't help feeling he is wrong, and that a human is, in some ways, superior to a fly, and The Kapital is more than a cow-pat.

'So, you must not love people. You must not love this world.'

'I mustn't?'

'Because people are imperfect. And this world is wrong too. Both need putting right. You must love people as they could be, not as they are. Better in a better world.'

'Yes?'

'But you must understand this about history . . . History consists of the lies of the winner. Because only the winner gets to tell the story. And the winner can write it however he wants. So he can make the past just as he wants it — not as it was, but as it ought to be.'

'Really?' I say.

'So the first task of the politician is to win. Because only if he wins can he put everything right. The past, the present as well as the future.'

Then the Boss starts to explain *people* to me.

He says there are four broad types of people. Firstly, there are people who need to exist, because they contribute to the good of us all. These are a tiny minority. They are leaders, artists, scientists who make the world a better place.

Then, there are the great majority of people who do no good and do no harm. And so are no use at all. It does not matter if they live or not. And so they are expendable. Because their fate makes no material

145

difference. It does not matter if they live in Minsk, work in a labour camp, or get their brains blown out against a wall.

Then, there are the enemy. The enemy of the proletariat, who need to be purged. They need to be removed for the good of us all.

The Boss says there are two types of person to be removed. There are those who should not exist. And there are those who should never have existed. Because they leave a trail, a memory. And so their evil lives on. After they are dead.

So, there are some people you can simply remove, rub out. But others you must *disinvent*.

'Disinvent?'

'Dismention. Disremember. Disdiscuss. Dishonour. Disrespect. Discredit. Disdain. Disphotograph. Dispaint. Disreference. Disrecognise. Disdiscover. Dispatch. Dismember . . .'

'Yes?'

'Remove every last trace. Any old fool can remove someone. In a moment. But it takes work and craft and time to disinvent them. To make what existed disappear without trace. Every day we have new lists. Page upon page. We have to disinvent thousands.'

'Thousands?' I ask. 'Thousands of what?'

'People.'

'Why?' I ask.

'Article 58 of the Criminal Code. And Article 32. Article 12. They all insist we do it. And it is no easy thing, either.'

'No?'

'They may be disinvented, but they still leave a mess behind them. A mess for others to clean up . . . '

'Oh.'

'And it's not just people. We will have to disinvent all manner of things.'

'What else, then?'

'Religion, the family, love . . . ' the Boss says.

'Is love *bad*, then?' It's news to me.

'Love is the worst evil.'

'Are you sure?'

'Love is the joker, the chaotic wildcard in the pack. The great disorganiser. It is glue. It is the sticky stuff that clogs the machine. It ties people together but the wrong people, in the wrong ways. It has no political purpose. It takes no heed of history. It has no sense of class-conflict. It lacks all morality. It works without reason. It feels without permission. It thinks the unthinkable. It speaks out of turn. It forgives everything. It embraces the unsuitable. It joins the incompatible. It promises the impossible. It revels in its own madness. It gives not a jot for the Party. It swears good is bad. It says black is white. It rolls around yelping and moaning. It tears off its clothes, to flaunt itself naked, at the flimsiest pretext. It spreads its legs to total strangers. It infects the old as well as the young. No one is safe from contamination. It spreads like the most virulent infection. But you cannot inoculate against it. You cannot ban it by law, or scare it away. You cannot even stick it against a wall and blow its brains out.'

'Maybe so . . . ' I say. I guess I'm too young to know.

'So we must stop the people *loving*. At least stop them loving each other . . . '

'Really?'

'And we must stop them thinking too. *Thinking* can be every bit as bad as *loving*.'

'Yes?'

'Ideas are more powerful than guns. We would not let everyone have guns, why should we let them have ideas?'

10

Decline

I saw the Boss getting sicker by the day. I observed, from our mealtime contacts, he was suffering frequent fainting fits, and daily growing a stranger to his memory.

There were poor days and worse days.

At his worst, he'd pause for ages between sentences. He'd pass out for minutes on end. Maybe, frozen in some gesture, with his fork poised in mid-air, on an arc to his mouth, or with an emphatic pointed finger. Then he'd sit stock still, or slump, with his eyes closed.

Then he'd blink, open his eyes again, suddenly alert, and continue as if nothing had happened.

Papa had treated an ancient rhino called Nestor for this condition. Sometimes the beast would be alert and frisky. Sometimes slow and forgetful. Sometimes he would topple over without warning, with a perplexed look to his cloudy eyes. Papa said it was called *vascular dementia*. It came and it went. It was all a matter of his arteriosclerosis, his coronary plumbing, and the amount of blood pumping through to his brain.

One day at lunch the Boss is served an unripe banana and bellows his outrage.

He demands that the *Minister for Buying Bananas* be sacked forthwith and put on trial. 'I daresay he has taken some bribe to defraud the State. Meanwhile he sits at home and gorges himself on *ripe* bananas, at our expense.'

But, there being no Minister exclusively dedicated to banana purchase, the message goes out to sack the Minister for Trade instead.

★ ★ ★

You do not have to be a veterinarian, or Elephantologist, to see that he's unwell. He is strangely quiet, slow and low in spirits. He keeps tapping his head with the palm of his right hand, as if trying to work something loose.

We've just started playing our first game of draughts. We're two moves in when he slumps sideways on his sofa. Spittle trickles from the left corner of his mouth.

His eyes seem unfocused and wander drunkenly. The left and right eyes take separate tours around the room.

He has a face of two halves. The right side

is firm and taut, but the left is slack, collapsed on itself, sagging like melting wax. His lips have taken a bluish tinge. They twitch and blow frothy bubbles of spit.

'Feels . . . ' he slurs, then trails off. ' . . . Sdrange.'

'Drunk?' I guess.

He shakes his head.

'Unhappy?' I ask.

He shakes his head again.

'Ill?' I guess.

He nods. 'Is right . . . ' he says. 'Is my . . . '

'Legs?'

'Noooo,' he says. I guess he means 'No'.

'Heart?'

'Noooo.' He blows a long sausage-shaped bubble of saliva from the corner of his mouth.

'Head?'

'Yesss . . . ' he agrees. 'Isss my head . . . '

I help the Boss to sit himself upright. I put the pillows behind his back. You don't have to be a Cordate Neurologist to know what's going on.

There is so much I want to tell him and, because I am nervous, it all comes out in a rush.

'I know what's wrong with you, old man,' I say. 'Because my Papa taught me all about mammalian brains, the *cross-over of function*, and the left and right cortex . . . '

The Boss looks at me oddly. As if I'm not there. He's not himself. He's lost and bemused.

'There's worst news and then there's better news,' I console him. 'Which would you rather hear first?'

His head sags to the left.

'Worst news — you're having a *stroke*,' I explain. 'There's a blockage or bleed in your brain. On the *right* hemisphere. It controls the left-hand side of your body, which is why it feels so weak on that side . . .

'Better news, the left side of the brain is probably fine . . . At our zoo, the animals often make a good recovery from a stroke, especially larger mammals. They have big brains with spare capacity. They can often re-learn all the things they need to know.'

'This . . . ' he taps his chest with his right hand, 'this here . . . ' His left eye swivels downwards. His right eye is glazed and looks straight ahead to the far distance.

There is a white corner of paper poking out from underneath his lapel. It belongs to an envelope in his inside pocket which I pull out. I believe he wants me to have it.

He nods. 'Take it . . . ' he slurs.

I fold the envelope and stuff it into my side trouser pocket. I barely have time to read the writing, in his hand, in green ink, on the cover. So, I hardly notice what it says —

The last testament of Josef Petrovich Iron-Man General Secretary of the Central Committee naming his successor

'It's important?' I ask.

He nods.

'Who shall I give it to?'

His eyes roll two ways.

'Bruhah?' I ask.

The right side of his face crumples in pain. But the left stays unconcerned. He leaks a shrill wail of distress.

'Krushka?'

He closes his eyes. He half-scowls, with the working side of his face. He gives a weary shake of his head.

I mention Malarkov, then Bulgirov, but he signals 'no' to both of them.

Then he holds out his left hand and extends one finger. I guess he wants to play charades.

'One word?' I guess.

He nods and extends a second finger.

'Two syllables?' I say.

He grunts, then holds out four fingers and a thumb.

'Five characters?'

He nods. Then laboriously, with the index finger of his left hand, he draws each character in turn in the air.

V . . . I . . . S . . . L . . . O . . . V . . .

'Volsiv?' I say. But I'm only joking.

He shakes his head wildly.

'Vislov?' I say.

He nods twice, then his eyes flicker closed.

So, he wants me to give the letter to someone called Vislov, whoever he is, when he's at home.

The Boss's head flops forward, with his eyes closed, and his chin resting on his chest. But I can tell from the throb in his wrist that he's still alive, with a busy pulse of over 110 beats per minute.

'Enough games, old man . . . ' I say. 'You need medical attention. And as soon as possible. From a doctor, or a veterinarian, or someone like that . . . '

11

Remember Lenin

I'll tell you a further, strange thing. Another of those curious coincidences that just happen in this special place — the Iron-Man's dacha — where the laws of nature are different to those in the outside world, by order of his Iron-Will. No sooner does the Boss fall ill than I do too.

Normally, I'm strong and sound — aside from when I'm throwing fits. Papa says I have the constitution of a tin can. So, whenever I've been dropped off a roof, hit by a milk truck, sizzled by lightning, or run over by a tram, I get a bit dented, but I'm never crushed.

And yet, suddenly, I am feeling strangely dizzy. And I have a terrible, throbbing, brain-splitting headache.

My sight goes blurry. The white of my left eye has gone crimson, from a burst blood vessel.

It is as if I am bleeding, all over, inside. I have bruise marks, from the slightest pressure, on my chest, arms and legs.

I press a finger onto my ankle to test and, lo and behold, a blood-red print forms under the skin.

I've developed some strange bleeding disease. I am used to bleeding from the inside out. But, now, I am bleeding from the outside in.

Matryona and the guards carry me to her room. I lie on a couch for three whole days in a hellish, scalding place between sleep and wakefulness, squirming and moaning. Terrible sights and awful thoughts pass through my head.

Then, on the fourth day, my mind clears. I can stand. I can walk. The bruises are gone. Now my skin stays clear.

★   ★   ★

But the Boss fares worse. Marshal Bruhah charges around the house, as if he owns it, in a state of high excitement — wailing his concern here, and beaming his exhilaration there — informing all that the Boss is dying — barking orders and then howling his sorrows, by turns.

But the Boss, the old devil, proves tougher than we all supposed. For days, he hovers on the brink.

The doors to eternity are flung wide open

to receive him. And yet he refuses to shuffle the final footstep, over the threshold to the golden lights on the other side.

Then, he rallies. He gathers his strength. Within a week, he is talking again, and able to hobble about the room. But while he seems better physically, in himself, he seems far worse in his head. He seems in steep decline in his mind.

A stroke can wreak havoc. And there's some basic know-how, and solid facts, he seems to have lost, for the moment at least.

In some ways, I'm relieved. I keep worrying he'll ask for his letter back. The last will and testament. Now he's decided to carry on living.

And I would be very happy to give the envelope back to him, of course. For it is his, to do with quite as he wishes. Except, I hid it somewhere for safe-keeping. And I can't remember where.

And I don't know how to tell him I've lost it. And I fear he'll be angry, if he finds out. I worry it's *confidential*. Or, worse still, *important*.

But the Boss has lost the memory of many, many things. And the letter seems the least of it.

★   ★   ★

Papa told me about the studies of his great chum Professor Luria, the Psychologist, about how the human memory works and how it goes wrong.

Comrade Alexander Romanovich Luria shows we have different memories, housed in different rooms in the brain. There's a memory like a film, which is an endless record of the episodes of our life — of all we've done, where we've been and who we've seen. It's our personal memory of our lifetime's experience. We can watch it in our mind's eye and play it forward and backward.

And we have an entirely different memory, arranged like an encyclopaedia — called the Semantic Memory, the Book of Meanings — which contains our knowledge of the world, what's what, and how things work.

And, from the way he's talking, the poor Boss has suffered damage to both of his memories, and to his mind, all over. That's what happens when you disrupt the blood supply to the brain. Memories just shrivel up. Knowledge dies.

Now, you're stranded in the present. You've lost some stepping-stones to your past.

He's lost memories of his life, and he's lost memories of basic, general knowledge. And it means he doesn't understand things as well as he did before.

158

But, worse, some days the Boss doesn't seem able to remember anything new for more than a few minutes. Then we're back where we started.

★ ★ ★

But where there's a will there's a way. There's always a willing helper, if you're not too proud to ask.

The Boss has started to use me as an extra organ — as a spare brain and back-up memory — when his own lets him down. So instead of consulting his recollections, he enquires of me.

It is a secret between the two of us. And, because I am just a menial, who keeps to himself, he does not have to worry that the word will leak out.

He just whispers his questions into my ear, with his warm, damp, tobacco-stained breath, pressed to my ear, prickling inside.

This gives me nicotine-stained ear lobes. And, to stop the itching, I have to clean out the yellow, oily film every evening.

★ ★ ★

'Hello, smiley boy,' he says, 'I asked for them to bring you to me. In confidence, between

159

the two of us, I need you to remember some things for me. Is your mind free? . . . I would remember them for myself, but I have other things on my mind.'

'*Yuri*,' I remind him, 'my name is *Yuri*.'

'That's as may be . . . ' he says, 'but it is neither here nor there and does not concern me . . . What I need to know . . . what I need you to remember for me . . . in confidence . . . is the name of a place. It is in Asia, to the East of China. It consists of many islands. I believe it is what they call a *country*. It's known as the land of the rising sun . . . '

'That would be *Japan*, I think.'

'Japan.' He nods wisely. 'You are right. It was there all the time, on the tip of my tongue. And another thing . . . '

'Boss?'

'There's a wild animal, smaller than a lynx. Vicious, very sharp teeth . . . '

'Wolf? Fox?'

'Not those, you stupid boy.'

'Polecat?'

'Of course not, idiotnik . . . It has beautiful thick fur. It makes fine hats.'

'Sable?'

'*Sable*. Of course,' he snaps. 'Why didn't you say so the first time?'

★ ★ ★

160

He has become short-tempered and is always complaining about those around him who, so he says, are always tricking him, or letting him down.

'They are holding me prisoner,' he says. 'They are stopping me from doing my work.'

'Who?' I ask.

'*Thingy-kov*,' he says, 'Bruhah-*hoo-hah*, Bulgy-*whatsis-name* and *You-know-who*. The four of them. They're ganging up on me.'

'Are you sure?'

'And they won't let me shoot Andrey Myokan . . . Where's the sense in that?'

'They won't?'

'They say he's old and loyal . . . But, surely, that's a defence for a dog, not a man?'

I shrug.

'And they say I can't bomb Amerika.'

'Yes?'

'They say there'd be trouble. Maybe even a war . . .'

I nod in sympathy. I can see it from both points of view. But it isn't my place to take sides.

'We have our nuclear missiles, primed to go. We can reach the East coast of Amerika, and the West. We can incinerate New Angeles, Bostov, Los Francisco, San-Something-or-other and Modern York. But they stop me launching the rockets.'

161

'They must have their reasons,' I guess.

'And then I want to round up the Jews and send them to camps in The Cold Lands. But they won't even let me do that.'

'Really?' I say.

'They say the Jews can't *all* be poisoners, traitors and spies.'

'Yes?'

'How dare they refuse me? When I am Josef Iron-Man, General Secretary of . . . ' he pauses, swivelling his eyes upwards, straining to recall, ' . . . some very important thing, or another . . . ' he grimaces with the efforts of trying to arrest his memories, ' . . . and Chairman of a very special whatchamacallit, even senior to that . . . '

But suddenly he's distracted again. Something has captured his attention in the corner of the room.

'What's that?' he demands, pointing accusingly. He's singled out the leather armchair for suspicion, and special interrogation.

'Well, that's a seat,' I say. 'A swivel chair.'

'What's it for?'

I oblige him. I sit in it to show him. I swing myself through a full circle.

'Bravo,' he claps. 'Well steered. I can see you've driven that one before.' He seems amazed at the rotations. 'Magnificent engineering.' He claps his hands to applaud the armchair. 'This is why Socialist Design leads the world. This is why we shall be first into space.' He chuckles at the cleverness of it all. He swivels the seat back and forth with his hand. 'Whatever will they think of next?

'And that,' he says, pointing to the desk. 'What's that?'

'A globe,' I say, 'a model of the world, spinning on its axis.'

'The world is *round?*'

'So they say.'

'I should have been told.' He frowns. '*The Ministry for Round Things* should have kept me informed . . . '

Shortly, he's hobbling up and down, muttering under his breath. He is waving with his hands, addressing the empty room on his pressing political concerns, as if rehearsing a speech.

'I am angry with . . . *those people*,' he declares. 'The scum . . . the vermin . . . they are the enemies of all the *other* people . . . These people need expelling from the Party, taking out of their jobs, evicting from their homes, separating from honest, decent people. They need putting in work camps. Some people need to suffer, to pay their debts to the Motherland, to make restitution. I do not care a jot if they all die in the process. I do not care if it ignites a war, to end all wars, with Amerika. Because it is the war that must surely come . . . It will be the culmination of history . . . '

'Who are they, these people?' I ask. '*The doctors?*'

'No.' He tastes the word for its sense and rejects it. 'Not the *doctors*.'

'*The Zionists?*' I guess. I've heard him complain about those before.

'Not the Zionists, either. Though they are bad enough.'

I shrug. I can't help him. I can't remember either.

'It is a terrible thing to hate people so much, so completely, so implacably, and totally without pity.' He observes the injustice. 'And yet not be able to remember their name . . . '

'I'm sure.'

'Because when you can't name them . . . you can't command they get shot . . . ' His gravelly voice is weary. He shakes his head in dismay. 'But I can't recall, *precisely*, who they are . . . These wasters. These reactionary bastards, these parasitical worms, these scum, this human effluence, this waste of flesh, this garbage, this swarm of flies on a shit-heap, these writhing rats in a rotting horse carcass, I only remember I hate them. Despise them. Loathe them. They are vermin.

164

They are excrement . . . Better to shoot the lot of them than to suffer having them amongst us any longer . . . And all the while they are a cancer eating away at our core . . . '

'But how can you hate them so much, when you don't know who they are?'

'I hate and despise them,' he fixes me with his still brown eyes, and wags a finger, 'with all sincerity, with all my will, my heart, and all my intellect, for the good of the people, to protect the progressive onward movement of history, to safeguard the advances secured by the Revolution, to protect the rights of the proletariat, and *for many more strong Socialist reasons* . . . '

'Yes?'

'But for the moment . . . ' He winces. He looks disconcerted, and shame-faced. 'I cannot recall what names these people use, who they are. But I know I have the best of reasons to hate them. That they are good and true ideological reasons, free of personal sentiment, founded in the truths of Marx, Engels and . . . ' He struggles to remember. 'Who's that *other* one . . . ?'

'Do you mean *Lenin*?'

'Yes, yes . . . ' He smiles, recalling an old friend. 'Remind me. What's dear old Lenin doing these days? We haven't seen him around for a while.'

'Isn't he dead?' I ask.

At school they always taught us he died back in 1924.

'Vladimir Ilyich Ulyanov is *dead*?' The Boss's voice quavers, his chest heaves. Moisture rolls out from the folds of his old walrus eyes, and trickles down his leathered cheeks in winding rivulets, into his whiskers. 'Why wasn't I told?' he demands.

★ ★ ★

I think back. I try to count how many days I have been here in the dacha and separated from Papa. Thirteen days, or fourteen? I'm not sure.

Time flows unevenly here, speeding crazily like quick-silver, then slowing, and thickening to cloggy lumps. And all the days of the week feel much the same. Every new day shakes us weary and bleary, too early from our beds, to descend the white waters of the Boss's moods.

Then, at the end, we celebrate. It's another day survived. And every night ends with a drunken feast.

12

The Last Supper

The Phoenix rises.

The next day, it's back like the old days. It's how things were at the best of times, before the Boss's recent illness. The Man of Iron rises at eleven and takes a light breakfast of fruit, eggs and bread. By midday he is in his limousine, speeding to the Palace of the People.

It's reported that he has a private meeting with the Argentine Ambassador, Manuel Bravo, then works in his office, meeting a range of dignitaries and officials, until eight o'clock when the Magnates and the Boss take themselves to the kinema downstairs in the Palace. They enjoy *You Can't Take It With You*, by the Yankee director Frank Capra.

The Boss's projectionist, Ivan Sanchin — a thin, nervous man in a boiler-suit, who has never been known to utter a word — screens the film together with Minister for Kinema, Ivan Bolshakov, who, as always, is in attendance to explain the kinematic details and translate, and to suffer abuse, and receive threats to his life, if the film proves a disappointment.

Because the usual Boss, the real Boss, is really unwell, recovering from his stroke, and can't distinguish right from left, or say what number follows nine, or remember that Lenin is dead, or who is President of the USA, his part has been played for the whole day by his very top stand-in, Comrade Director Dikoy, who has been given permission to stare, scowl or grunt freely, and to talk lightly and within reason — as the Great Leader Himself — so long as he sticks to simple chit-chat and pleasantries. But, come supper, back at the dacha, the true Boss, himself, is well enough disposed to oust his double, and attend in his own skin, and talk and drink and eat for himself.

* * *

It is an intimate gathering for the Boss — together with Bulgirov, Malarkov, Krushka and Bruhah — commencing just before midnight in the small dining room.

There is a Georgian buffet laid out on the side tables with tomato salad, vegetable pkhali, roast aubergine, khinkali, mtsvadi, kharcho, lobiani, chicken bazhe, khachapuri adjaruli, laid out under the watchful eyes of

Lakoba the guard and Matryona the house-keeper.

The Boss seems to have forgotten my role as his food-taster because he gets tetchy at my proper, timely involvement with his plates, sampling his food before him, with a quick spoonful here, and a fast fork stab there, and an occasional rapid finger dipped in the sauce, as a food-taster must.

So, he turns to me, smiling for all the company to see, and whispers his frank advice in my ear.

'Go fuck yourself,' he advises, 'imbecile child. And keep your greasy, grimy hands out of my dinner, or I'll have you sprinkled with rosemary and lemon juice, basted in pig fat, and spit-roasted, with an apple in your gawping gob.'

It puts shivers through me. It brings a smile to my face. I am strangely proud of him, all of a sudden. For the moment it sounds like the Boss is back to his old self again. You know he is on the mend, and at his best, when he is swearing freely and threatening clearly.

His mind is working well tonight. The blood must be flowing freely to his brain.

He starts talking business. He asks Bruhah how affairs are progressing with the arrested doctors. He wants to know if they have confessed yet to the charges of trying to murder the leadership of the Union of Socialist Republics.

He warns that the doctors must be broken. And quickly. They must confess to the murders of Shurpikov and of Zootziev, by medical malpractice. These doctors must also be Jewish. They must confess to being *Zionist-saboteur-doctors* in the pay of Amerikan Fascism.

All this must happen in time for their public trial shortly. And that if they are not broken quickly, the person in charge of their interrogation must himself be broken. And replaced by someone who can break doctors properly and quickly.

There are nuts to be cracked, says the Boss. So, where's the nutcracker?

One Head of the Ministry of State Security had been executed for delay and incompetence. Another could shortly follow.

Comrade Iron-Man says it is a simple matter. The interrogators must take their gloves off and cease being kind. They must beat the doctors. Beat them some more. Then beat them again. Break their bones. And grind them to dust.

'And *whatsisname*? That one who said I was ill, unfit to govern, and should retire?'

'Professor Weidermann,' says Bruhah. 'He has a long tongue. He tells us you have fainting spells. And suffer confusions.'

'Make sure he is beaten properly,' says the Boss, 'as properly as possible. More than once. Let him enjoy some confusions himself, and fainting spells too . . . '

'It's done,' Bruhah nods.

'And yet, we all grow older.' The General Secretary is solemn and looks balefully at his four assistants. 'And I do not know who might ever replace me, when that day finally comes, if my powers should ever wane . . . '

'The loving people love the Beloved Leader,' says Bruhah. 'No one could ever replace him.'

'He is the Gardener of Human Happiness,' says Krushka, 'he is the Great Uncle, the Kind Father and the Repository of all Our Dreams. The Genius. The Sun that Lights Our Day. He is loved by everyone, wherever he goes.'

'We all know the poem by heart,' Bruhah says. And he commences to recite —

O great Comrade Iron-Man,
Leader of all peoples,
Greatest of Philosophers.
The kindest of hearts.
Moral beacon to the cosmos.
Thou who fructifies the earth,
Thou who makest bloom the spring,
Thou, splendour of the seasons,

Companion of the planets,
O thou, Sun reflected by millions of hearts.

'Tell me,' says Krushka, 'was any other human being ever so loved and revered by his fellow man?'

'The General Secretary is in fine health at the peak of his powers,' observes Bruhah.

'The Comrade is irreplaceable,' says Krushka.

'You are rust-proof,' says Malarkov. 'You are truly the Man of Iron.'

'And you?' The Boss looks to Bulgirov, who has stayed awkwardly silent, wearing a vague, weary expression, peering into the distance over the rims of his gold-framed spectacles. 'What's your name again?'

'Bulgirov,' says Bulgirov, surprised that his close colleague for these past fifty years now cannot remember his name.

'Well, Bulgirov, could you replace me, you flea-ridden old bird, you bag of shit and feathers?'

'No, Comrade,' says Bulgirov, 'I do not have your wisdom, kindness, vigour or authority.'

'And you are an old, worm-ridden, rotting carcass, aren't you? Like Motolov.'

'As you say,' Bulgirov murmurs, leaks a thin smile and nods politely.

'And Koretski is a Jew and a Yankee sympathiser . . . And *you-know-who* is a fraudster and liar. And *whatsisname* is a moron.'

'He is?' asks Malarkov.

'And Bruhah here is a Mingrelian, a foreigner, and a rapist. So, he has to poke his prick into anything that moves, including his colleagues' wives. And is known to eat his own children . . . '

'Koba?' Bruhah protests.

'And poor Krushka, here, is a country bumpkin who can barely spell his name. He's never opened a book in his life and can't count past five. And is only fit to run a slaughterhouse . . . '

Krushka reddens. A deep hurt shows on his face. But he keeps his lips zipped.

'So, where does that leave us?'

The inadequates look down and away. They stay silent.

'Some of you think you can ride on past glories. That you are safe and secure in your puffed-up positions. But it is not so. No one is safe. No one is above judgement. Even the highest can be cast down low . . . '

The four look at the Boss, with silent, suffering dignity. They remind me of the wolf pack at The Kapital Zoo, sitting patiently in a circle, waiting to be fed. Each knows his place in the pack. Each knows there will be more than enough to eat. Especially if they get lucky, and catch the keeper off guard.

Then the Boss turns to me.

'Enough business. We'll play a game. *Act the Animal.* Yuri, here, goes first. Let's choose his task . . . '

He dips his hand into his upturned Marshal's hat, draws out a ball of paper, opens and smooths the slip, and reads the chosen task.

'Yuri,' he commands, 'you are Sergei's Fox Terrier. You must run around the table twice, on all fours, barking as you go, then sniff. Andrei's arse, and then lick Nikita's face. Then try to hump the table leg. And don't forget to wag your tail as you go . . . '

Sometimes, you think he wants to make people look smaller and lower than they really are. Because he then gets Malarkov to be a house mouse in the skirting, and Bruhah to be a maggot in a piece of rotten meat, who then turns into a horse-fly.

*   *   *

And so we carry on into the early hours. There is more Georgian wine. More games. There is arm-wrestling. There is singing. There is more Georgian wine. There is brandy. Malarkov falls asleep at the table and is made to do a

174

forfeit of drinking seven glasses of vodka, after which he promptly wets himself.

Krushka falls flat on his face while dancing and is made to drink a bottle of Finnish cloudberry liqueur.

The Boss paces himself with his drinking and stays more alert than his minions. He watches them with wry amusement and, at intervals, pulls their strings and has them dance like puppets.

At four in the morning he tires of it all and declares the gathering is at an end.

It is Sunday, but he warns them he will phone them early. He advises them to rush home and enjoy a few hours' sleep before their day's work begins all over again.

The chauffeurs are summoned from the kitchen, and the limos draw up, churning the gravel, at the main entrance. Malarkov and Bruhah share a car, as they often do. Krushka travels with Bulgirov.

The guard Isakov sees the Boss to his chamber of choice. This night he has selected the room just along from the small dining room which he has not used for several days.

When he returns from seeing the Boss to his room, Isakov announces to the other guards, 'The General Secretary said this — 'I'm going to bed. Stand down. I shan't be needing you. You can go to bed too.''

'He told us to *stand down?*' asks Lakoba, Captain of the Guard.

'He did.'

'*Go off duty?*'

'Indeed.'

'Well,' says Lakoba, 'I've never heard him say that before. Not once in seven years.'

'He must be feeling generous,' says Isakov. 'He told us all to take a good rest. He said he wouldn't be needing us again.'

13

The Mystery of the Sealed Room

Next morning, we all know something is amiss. But we don't know what. And we haven't a clue what to do.

I'm waiting to be called for the Boss's breakfast. But the call never comes.

The whole household knows where Comrade Iron-Man, Great Father, had laid down his head to sleep the night before. He'd chosen Living Room 3. Everyone has been warned to make no noise in that vicinity.

There are sensors in the soft furnishings of all the rooms. Those in that chamber signalled movement to the guard room, several times in the early hours, as the Boss tossed and turned on his sofa-bed. But now they have fallen silent.

The staff huddle outside in the corridor. Matryona, the housekeeper, stands by the small oval table where she has placed the breakfast tray. She lays a testing finger on the coffee pot and clucks. Now it's too cool, and needs replacing.

Ten o'clock, no movement.

Eleven, still no movement.

Midday. Nothing.

The guards, either side of the door, make silent comments, raising their brows, rolling their eyes, shrugging. It is later than the General Secretary ever sleeps and yet he isn't risen.

Matryona has pressed an ear to the door, and to the connecting wall in the adjacent room but can hear no movement. I am waiting in the corridor to be invited in to taste his breakfast. My belly has started rumbling, for the Boss's breakfast is my breakfast. But I can't start without him.

None of the guards can risk disturbing him. The General Secretary expressly forbids it. He has told his contingent of guards he will shoot anyone who enters his room without an invitation. He is a man of his word. And he recently disposed of his secretary and bodyguard after they had given him twenty years' loyal service.

All afternoon, we are gathered in the corridor — Matryona, myself, two guards outside the door, and a further two at the entrance to the garden, a maid, and Pavel, the Boss's new secretary.

Other staff come and go. They press ears to the door and walls. They strain to hear. They shake their heads. They shrug. There are no signs, clues or indications.

At three o'clock the four members of the guard grow bold and draw lots. The plan is simple. Whoever draws the shortest match will ring the Leader's room from the telephone in the main hall. Everyone has access to that phone. It will not draw suspicion on the guards. The caller will hang up as soon as there is any answer. The other three are sworn to secrecy. All will deny making the call.

If pressed, they will swear it was Dmitry the chauffeur. He is a surly and uncomradely individual. He is not married. He has no children. If it comes to the worst, and he has to be sacrificed for the good of all, he will not be so missed as any of the others.

Outside the Comrade's room, we can hear the call. The phone rings loud inside. It rings on and on. But no one answers.

Although the Comrade is rust-proof, a Man of Steel, invincible and well-nigh immortal, those gathered outside his door look concerned.

We are very worried for him. We worry for ourselves if anything bad should happen to him. There is trouble if we do nothing. There is trouble if we do anything. Only the Leader's quick temper, and readiness to punish, prevents us all from forcing an entry.

The afternoon shadows lengthen. The

guard changes, having served their day's stint. The floodlights are turned on outside. We hear the staff bus scatter the gravel as it turns to take the day shift back to The Kapital.

At ten o'clock, as every night, the last package of mail arrives from the Palace of the People. This carries important documents and details matters of immediate concern.

The Boss always insists that this postal delivery is brought into him, without ceremony or delay, whatever he is doing.

Now, at last — twelve hours after our first concern — we have permission. It's safe to go in.

Lakoba, Captain of the Guard, orders Solitov in to deliver the package of mail.

The door is unlocked and swings open. From the doorway, I can see the Boss sprawled out on the parquet floor.

He is lying in a pool of liquid. It must be his own pee. He is wearing a white vest and long woollen underpants. There's a copy of *The Daily Truth* at his side.

I see his watch lies besides him, the glass broken. It reads 6.30.

He raises his right hand.

'Dzz . . . ' he says. 'Dzz . . . '

The Boss looks red in the face, going on purple around the lips, dazed and very angry.

Matryona announces that his skin is very

cold to the touch. He is in some kind of stupor. He cannot talk clearly. His eyes do not focus. It's an easy guess. He's had another stroke.

Tomsky the guard and Matryona lift him up and carry him to the sofa, next door, in the small dining room. It is warmer there and there is more space and fresher air.

Lakoba tells Solitov to ring the Ministry of State Security.

When they get Yubiov, the Minister, on the line he says they must ring Bruhah and Malarkov and take their orders from them.

They ring Malarkov. He says, 'Do nothing.' He will ring them back.

Half an hour later Malarkov rings back. He tells them he cannot get hold of Bruhah. But he tells them to stand by the phone, and wait for further instructions.

Half an hour later, Bruhah rings.

'Don't tell anyone the Boss is ill,' he says. 'I will be there shortly, to see for myself.'

At three in the morning, Bruhah arrives with Malarkov. They go in to see the Boss lying on the sofa in the dining room. Malarkov looks terrified. He pauses to take off his squeaking boots, and carries them under his arm, so as not to disturb the Boss. But Bruhah looks relaxed and cheerful.

'Ah,' says Bruhah, gazing down on Comrade Iron-Man, 'what's the panic? Can't you see the Comrade is taking a nap? He is sleeping peacefully. He must be very tired . . . '

Then Bruhah and Malarkov turn about and are gone.

Nobody knows what to do. The guard daren't defy Bruhah. It's not their task to make the decisions.

At eight o'clock Krushka appears, looking sheepish. He doesn't go in to see the Boss but, hearing he's poorly, orders us to call in the doctors.

And not before time, because Comrade Iron-Man has been lying there without medical help for more than a day.

★   ★   ★

It takes thirty-three minutes for Modern Medicine to arrive and, when it finally comes, it comes loud and in force, with sirens, bells and flashing lights, in a convoy of vans, ambulances and cars, spilling out a crowd of doctors and nurses. They are neatly labelled by their lapel badges as Cardiologists, Anaesthetists, Thoracic Surgeons, Neurologists, Ear-Nose-and-Throat Specialists, Ophthalmologists. In their wake come technicians pushing mobile x-ray machines and life support systems.

The doctors crowd the room. But they are strangely hesitant. No one seems to want to lay the first finger on the sick man.

'Please, Comrade Professor, will you make the initial examination?'

'Please, Comrade Colleague, I believe a Cardiologist should examine first . . . '

'No, observe the Petrov Reflex. Surely, a Neurologist is needed here . . . '

Then the heavyweights spy a junior dentist, lurking at the door, and order him to chance his arm by making the first incursion.

He's told to remove the patient's false teeth to free the airwaves. But his hands are shaking so violently he spills the dentures on the floor, then stamps on them by mistake, sending pink and white splinters of mastic cascading across the tiles.

Professor Luvetsky comes forward. He says they must take off the patient's shirt and measure his blood pressure. They cut the clothes away with scissors.

The pulse is 78 beats per minute but faint. The blood pressure is 190 over 110. His right side seems paralysed. They agree he's had a catastrophic stroke from a bleed in the left hemisphere.

He is given a 10 per cent solution of magnesium sulphate, and a camphor injection. They place four leeches behind each of his ears.

An hour later they apply a kaolin poultice

to his neck, and increase the dose of leeches to six on each side. But it is still not enough to restore the Great Man.

Bruhah and Malarkov let it be known that the doctors must first clear any further medical procedures with them.

The doctors advise that the General Secretary is dying of a massive stroke. It is a matter of days not weeks.

★ ★ ★

I have not been allowed close. I'm watching it all from a distance, in the corridor. But I can't help thinking that events are following a curious course.

The Boss is seriously ill but they have left him a day before calling for any medical treatment.

Bruhah has taken it upon himself to instruct everyone in their tasks — including even Krushka, Bulgirov and Malarkov.

Isakov, who was one of the dacha guards, has become Bruhah's confidential shadow, padding behind him everywhere, taking his orders, and bossing his former colleagues, as if suddenly promoted.

While the doctors are struggling to save the General Secretary's life, Bruhah and two of his assistants from Internal Affairs are clearing the Boss's office, examining every single sheet of paper. Shredding some and filing others. You sense they are looking for something particular.

All this serves to remind me of the Boss's final letter. The one he calls his *last testament*. And I wonder again where I left it. For now would be the time to produce it. I don't want to conceal it. But I don't want to admit I have lost it.

Bruhah's chauffeur collects the boxes of papers and returns at hourly intervals for the next load.

Meanwhile Bruhah is interviewing the dacha guards and reassigning them to new duties, posting them out in distant directions, far away from The Kapital. As if they won't be needed here any more.

Lakoba asks to stay at the dacha, near the family home, since his wife is about to deliver their baby. But he is offered a choice of 'here' — Bruhah stamps the ground — or a transfer to Minsk. So he opts for Minsk, instead of burial, without further argument.

The Boss is still alive but already his household is being disbanded while he lies on his sickbed.

People don't expect him to live.

★　★　★

Bruhah is in a wildly excitable state. He is exhilarated by the Boss's sickness, then fearful at any flickering sign of recovery.

When Comrade Iron-Man shows any fleeting sign of returning strength — opening his eyes, muttering in his stupor, turning his head towards visitors — Bruhah fawns upon him, kneeling by the bedside, kissing his hand, coaxing him — 'Dear Comrade Secretary, promise us, you will never leave us . . . '

But, as long as the Boss lies silent, failing in his coma, Bruhah looks to him with contempt and speaks to him with condescension — 'Koba, make up your mind. What are you doing in life? Are you coming or going?'

And, to pass the time, he starts telling him jokes —

It is an international athletics competition. A Slav runner is talking to other competitors — an Amerikan, a Romanian, a German and a Swiss.

'Excuse me,' the Swiss asks, 'but what is your opinion of the current meat shortage?'

But everyone frowns. They shake their heads in confusion. For no one understands the question.

The Amerikan says, 'What's a 'shortage'?'

The German says, 'What is 'excuse me'?'
The Romanian says, What is 'meat'?'
And the Slav says, 'What is 'opinion'?'

'Here is another one, Koba.' Bruhah taps the Comrade's shoulder. 'A joke about you . . . '

Early in the morning, Comrade Iron-Man arrives at his office and opens his window. He sees the sun and says, 'Good morning, dear Sun!'
The sun replies, 'Good morning, dear Josef!'
The Comrade works, and then at noon he heads to the window and says, 'Good afternoon, dear Sun!'
The sun replies, 'Good afternoon, dear Josef!'
In the evening, the General Secretary calls it a day, and heads once more to the window, and says, 'Good evening, dear Sun!'
But the sun has fallen silent now. So Comrade Iron–Man says again, 'Good evening, dear Sun! What's the matter with you?'
And the sun says, 'You can go kiss my arse, shorty. I'm in the West now.'

'What do you think, Koba?' Bruhah stabs the chest of the comatose General Secretary. 'I hear people tell it on the streets. Good joke, or bad?'

★　★　★

But there's a stranger turn of events than that.

Yubiov, Minister of State Security, has used his initiative.

Without consulting Bruhah or Krushka, he has searched out the very top doctors in the land — those that had treated Comrade Iron-Man in the past. He tracks them down to the cells of The Freedom and Peace Prison.

He finds they are being held by his Ministry, and being interviewed, under duress and with menaces, in order that they will confess to their conspiracy — to murder the leaders of the State.

Yubiov has them released, now he needs them all of a sudden, to treat the General Secretary.

They have been washed down, tidied up, bandaged over, fed, clothed and comforted, but they look a sorry, demoralised bunch. You sense that their hearts aren't in the task of saving their tormentor, and their capacities are diminished.

It's chilling to see them. They have suffered for their profession as doctors. They treated the Boss. And so did Papa.

Our nation's leading Neurologist has lost his front teeth, upper and lower. The lenses of his spectacles are cracked, blurring his vision. He has developed the kind of rapid facial tick he used to treat in others. He has taken to squealing quietly to himself, under his breath, every few seconds, as if he's impersonating a terrified mouse.

The Professor of Cardiac Surgery has a black, paddle-shaped left hand. For all the fingers have been crushed and flattened with a hammer. One of his eyes is closed completely, swollen purple like a plump ripe plum, so it looks as if he's engaged in a monstrous, playful wink. Both his arms jerk. He is unsteady on his feet.

The ear-nose-and-throat specialist has fared worse than the other two. He arrives on a stretcher, lain on a gurney, bandaged in white crepe, from neck to thigh, with an oxygen mask taped to his black and purple face. Although he cannot actively examine the patient himself, it is thought he may be able to contribute to the general discussion and make some useful observations lying down, in his wide-awake moments.

The two walking wounded examine the

patient as best they can. They do not seem optimistic when Bruhah challenges them.

'Which of you,' he demands, 'will guarantee the life of Comrade Iron-Man?'

'He is dying,' says the Cardiologist. 'It's too late. There's a massive bleed in his brain. It's been left too long. There's no saving him. But . . . '

'But what?' barks Bruhah.

'He is coughing up blood.'

'So?'

'He is suffering a severe stomach haemorrhage.'

'Well?'

'This does not indicate a stroke as primary cause. It indicates that something else caused the bleeding — in both the stomach and brain.'

'Yes?'

'It indicates poisoning.'

'*Poisoning?*'

'From a blood-thinning agent . . . Like Warfarin, say . . . '

'Surely,' Bruhah glares, 'you must be mistaken.'

'And now he is drowning, slowly.'

'Drowning?' asks Bruhah.

'In his own blood — collecting in his lungs.'

★ ★ ★

If appearances are anything to go by, this drowning in your own blood is a very unpleasant and slow way to die. From the doorway, I watch the Iron-Man's face undergo grotesque gurning, while he mutters and whimpers.

At intervals he seems to briefly recover consciousness. Then he casts evil, threatening looks on those around him.

Once he lifts his hand and points one digit upwards. But we do not understand. If it is a profound gesture. To the heavens. Or an earthly observation, showing us all the finger.

⋆ ⋆ ⋆

The next morning, I duck under the outstretched arm of a guard and get into the treatment room. I've decided to see it all for myself, close up.

You'd never guess.

It's unbelievable. But true.

Honestly. Trust me.

The patient, the man on the gurney, is not Comrade Iron-Man.

Anyone should be able to see.

He is younger, at least seven centimetres taller. With different, fleshy ears. And deeper scars on his face. His unwebbed feet, with unfused toes, reach the steel bar at the end of the trolley.

I can see the patient's profile clearly.

Then I burst into tears.

For I see the features of my good-friend Felix. Poor, dear Felix. Conjurer, joker, discoverer of eggs in strangers' ears.

His face is frozen, and oddly reddened.

'He is close to the end,' I hear a nurse whisper.

'He looks so different . . . ' says the red-eyed, blotchy-faced, straggly-haired, sniffy lady at the foot of the trolley, smearing the tears on her powdered cheek with the back of her gloved hand. 'So strange. Unrecognisable. Like a different man. Older yet younger . . . And, when he looks at me, it's as if he just doesn't know me . . . '

We know she is Nadezhda, the Boss's daughter, summoned to her Papa's bedside, before it is too late.

The twitchy man by her side with the glazed eyes is Viktor, the Boss's son. He is unsteady. He sways forward and back, muttering in slurred undertones, 'You've killed him, you bastards . . . You evil, fucking, murderous bastards . . . '

Everyone knows Viktor. He's a man of dark moods, and drunk as usual — even called to his father's deathbed.

He fears his father will interrogate him on his job as Air Force Commander of the

Kapital Military District. He fears difficult questions, and so comes armed with files of correspondence, figures and weather maps.

I won't disturb the Great Man's children by telling them directly what they should see for themselves. But they need to be told. The world needs to know. The truth must be told. There's some awful mistake at work here.

★   ★   ★

Then the sick man takes his last rasping breath, and turns the final corner — to become the dead man. And someone says it —

'He's gone.'

Then wails go up, overlaid by gasps, whimpers, blubbers and murmurs.

The gathering laments the Iron-Man's passing.

Myself, I weep for a better man. I cry for Felix.

By some unwritten rule, those gathered form a line behind the son and the daughter. And take their turn to kiss the dead man, some on his cheeks, some on his forehead and some on his hand.

Bruhah bustles in front of the other grandees, to be the first amongst equals.

I turn from the doorway and walk to

Krushka who is standing beside Malarkov, whispering to his ear.

'Uncle Nikita,' I tell him. 'Don't worry yourself. There's some terrible mistake. That's not the Boss on the gurney.'

'Shhh,' he whispers. He frowns. He looks around in alarm.

'It's a double.'

'A double?'

'It's my friend Felix Oussopov. He's a magician . . . and clown . . . from Yekaterinburg. That's not Comrade Iron-Man . . . '

'How can that be?' Krushka asks. 'And how can you know?'

I list the evidence — the unfused toes, the length of the body, the shape of the ears, the scars on the face.

He nods. He pats my head. 'Poor child,' he observes. 'What are we going to do with you? You see it all. Yet you understand nothing.' Then he steps backward.

And the conversation ends there and then.

All of a sudden.

And all I remember, after, is that something heavy-handed happens behind my back.

It feels as though the weight of the Urals is falling upon my head. Before an elephant sits on my face. Then the world fades from grey to black.

14

A Message From the Other Side

I wake in another place.

I don't know how much time has passed. I am lying on a tiled floor, on a scatter of damp straw, with a stench of ammonia scorching my nostrils.

I have the mother of all headaches. My lower lip is sliced open where my teeth have sunk themselves in. The front of my trousers is sodden. I suppose I must have wet myself.

I am in a brick walled room, maybe five metres by four. There is a single barred window high in the wall. There is a door of a metal plate within a cast-iron frame. There is a spy hole and a small sliding partition. I guess it's a cell.

There is no light except the waning dusk through the small window.

There is a smell of drains and, lain on top of that, a ripe stench of rot.

In the far corner sits another figure, a companion, on his backside on the floor, hunched, head on his knees, looking downward, still and silent, and completely dejected.

'Hello,' I say, 'I'm Yuri.'

He doesn't turn to look my way. He doesn't even bother to reply.

I'm not one to force myself on another soul, or prattle away with unnecessary conversation. If he doesn't want to talk then that's his choice. So I wait several minutes before I address him again.

'Sorry to disturb you, Comrade,' I say, 'can you tell me where we are?'

There's no moving him. He stays resolutely immobile and silent.

He doesn't shift a millimetre. His chest doesn't move to his breath. He holds his head entirely still.

'Excuse me for asking,' I remark, 'but are you ill?'

As I step a few paces his way, the smell of rot gets stronger and richer. It prickles hard in the nose. Its putrid fingers reach up your nostrils and burn at the back of your throat. The stench is scorching.

Flies emerge buzzing, over the black sticky trickle down from his ear. He is grey-faced with a sunken-cheeked starved look.

His right hand seems strangely shaped, like a wooden paddle. Then I see he has lost the fingers, leaving blackened stubs with ivory buttons of bone sticking up. His mouth is splayed open, in an awkward, reluctant half-smile, showing mushy black gums and splintered white teeth.

His eyes are closed, but I sense something small but lively wriggling beneath, twitching the eyelid, maybe a worm or a bug.

When I reach to touch his shoulder there is no resistance. He feels strangely flimsy. Hollow. With parchment skin, and a body light as driftwood.

He topples over onto his side. But his limbs stay stiff, as they were. So he looks like a doll lain on its side, arms reaching out, legs at right angles to his body.

I see my companion's condition. He is starved. He is silent and still because he is dead, and — from the scent of him — he departed a while ago.

The straw is sparse on the floor, but I gather all I can to spread over the man. A mound of dirty straw is a better sight than a corpse. It's as close to burial as the resources allow.

★ ★ ★

On the second day I start to hear *the noise*.

click . . . click . . . click . . . click . . . click . . . click . . .

An endless metallic ticking. It is a distant tapping sound. It's quiet but insistent and repetitive. It comes from the water pipe, low down, to the side of the door.

To pass the time I start listening to the taps. There is no other entertainment. After a while, I start to count.

There are thirty-three, evenly spaced. Then there's a pause for many minutes. Then come thirty-three more. Then thirty-three more on top of that.

So I realise it's an intelligent human making the noise, and trying to communicate, and not some machine or random happening.

But why thirty-three?

I know I need to think scientifically, like a professor, the ways my Papa would. I try to work it out. It's good to have a task in mind. It prevents you from feeling low or badly treated.

So what's so special about thirty-three?

For a start, it's common knowledge, it's the atomic number of Arsenic.

Of course, it's also the sum of the first four positive factorials.

Everyone knows, it's the number of vertebrae in the human spine, up to the coccyx.

It goes without saying, it's the boiling point of water. On the Newton Scale.

According to Granny Anya, it was the age of Jesus Christ when he was crucified in AD 33.

And then, of course, there are thirty-three characters in the Cyrillic alphabet.

And thirty-three (.33) is the speed of a new

gramophone record in revolutions per minute.

I give it some thought and then I tap back. I tap on the metal water pipe with a five-kopeck coin I find in my pocket.

I give thirty-three taps, and the same number comes back promptly, from the other side.

So, now, we've got a conversation going. So I know I should say something different, yet to the point.

I go for this — three taps, pause, one tap, pause, four taps, pause, two taps.

Because, as any schoolboy knows, 3.142 equals *Pi*, the ratio of a circle's circumference to its diameter, to three decimal places.

Within a minute, I get a reply.

One tap, pause, six taps, one tap, eight taps.

It's then I know we're speaking the same language, because whoever it is has tapped back *Phi*, 1.618. A brother of *Pi*, and the number of the golden section.

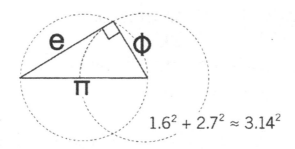

$$1.6^2 + 2.7^2 \approx 3.14^2$$

It's pure Pythagoras. As every geometry student knows.

But, just to make sure, I test again. I tap 1–4–9–16. The sequence of the square of numbers from one to four.

And sure enough, when the answer comes, it's twenty-five — the next number in the series.

Now, I'm as fond of numbers as the next boy. And I enjoy swapping as much as anybody. But there's a lot you just can't say with ordinals and cardinals. When it comes to feelings, you're maybe better off with words.

So now we're in the mood for a chat, we're looking for a code to let us start talking.

The tapper taps thirty-three. Then thirty-three again. So, I take a leap of faith, I guess what he means to say. He's telling me to use the alphabet.

It's a short leap of logic. And soon we're talking.

If you assign a number for the letter's order, you can spell 'Hello.'

Promptly, I answer him back —
HELLOTOYOUTOO

It is not original, but it progresses us from numbers to words, from noise to meanings.

He taps back —
IAMBEINGHELDPRISONERFULL-STOP

I say I think I'm a prisoner too. Because I'm being held by persons unknown, against my will. But I got knocked out, so I wasn't conscious when they dumped me in the cell.

He says —

IAMALLALONEINHERE

So I reply —

IVEGOTACOMPANIONBUTHEISDEAD-SOHESAYSNOTHINGANDSMELLSBAD-NOTTHATITSHISFAULT

But I don't mention he has insects wriggling under his skin and in his eyes and under the lids, and coming and going, through his nostrils and ears, as if they were stairways and tunnels and doorways.

He asks me what my crime is. So I tell him —

IAMGUILTYOFINNOCENCE

I say my mistake was being in the wrong place at the wrong time, and seeing things I should not see.

He says —

IAMGUILTYOFKNOWLEDGE

He says that his crime is similar to mine. It is knowing things that he should not know, and seeing things he should not have seen. Concerning important people.

He says it is good to talk to a kindred spirit after such long, long solitude.

I say that all this tapping is very long-winded. Is there not a quicker way of saying what you mean?

He says he's heard that, in the Gulag, they use a simple code.

It goes this way —

You form a grid of the thirty main characters, six across and five down —

А	Б	В	Г	Д	Е/Ё
Ж	З	И	К	Л	М
Н	О	П	Р	С	Т
У	Ф	Х	Ц	Ч	Ш
Щ	Ъ	Ы	Э	Ю	Я

Then each letter gets assigned a pair of taps. The first says the row, the second says its position in that row.

Easy. Once you know how.

1,1,	1,2	1,3	1,4	1,5	1,6
2,1	2,2	2,3	2,4	2,5	2,6
3,1	3,2	3,3	3,4	3,5	3,6
4,1	4,2	4,3	4,4	4,5	4,6
5,1	5,2	5,3	5,4	5,5	5,6

It doesn't take long.
You pick it up in no time.
Give or take the odd misspelling.
So, soon we're chattering away — like we've known each other all our lives.

We call it *The Citizen's Telephone*. I call him *Tappetty-Tap-Tap* or *The-hungry-man-on-the-other-side*.

He says he's been left to rot for eight days now, without anything to eat or drink.

I ask him his name.

He says —

IAMCOMRADENONAMEYOUBECOM-
RADENONAMETOO

For names are knowledge for them to beat out of us. If we do not know, we cannot say. Then, we cannot betray each other.

He says he's been held for two weeks, all told. They've given him a fearful kicking, pulled off some of his finger nails and knocked out some of his teeth. He thinks he may have gone deaf in one ear, from the beatings. But he can't tell them anything. He has nothing to tell.

★　★　★

I am not complaining. Obviously, I would rather have *The-hungry-man-on-the-other-side* to talk to than no one at all. He is a good man. A kind man. He is company. He means well. He has good advice on a wide range of subjects. He has a huge store of knowledge. But the way he tells it is always a little dull. And he does not have a funny or sunny nature. Or an optimist's view for the future of things.

He tends to linger on the dark side of life, and dwell on the worst that can happen.

Naturally, he's getting thirsty. He gets around to telling me that a person is better off drinking their own urine than nothing at all.

He further advises that insects are a rich source of protein, if nothing better presents itself. It's best to chew fast, then swallow faster. Thus maximising nutritional intake while minimising unpleasant after-taste, and preventing any little critter from trotting around in your insides — which is not pleasant for either party.

Anyway, he reassures, a healthy person can survive for long periods without much food, as long as he keeps hydrated.

He says I must change my attitude to insects and rodents, to stop dismissing them as vermin, and welcome them as nutrition instead. He surprises me by listing five good uses for a dead mouse which I never would have guessed at myself.

1. nutrition
2. hydration
3. ribs as needles
4. jawbone and teeth as a knife
5. tail as string

He advises that if my wounds from my interrogation go septic, I can put maggots on the open flesh to clean the wound, by nibbling away the infected bits.

He says that, when my captors are hurting me, I must always remind them of my name, and say I am a person, the same as them. This is not a perfect defence but it helps to remind them you are a human being, not garbage.

'Yes?' I say. 'Do you know any jokes?'

'Not any recent ones,' he says.

So I tell him this one, which Comrade Krushka, himself, told me —

Three workers find themselves locked up in prison, and they ask each other what they're in for. The first man says, 'I was always ten minutes late to work, so I was accused of sabotage.' The second man says, 'I was always ten minutes early to work, so I was accused of espionage.' The third man says, 'I always got to work exactly on time, so I was accused of having a contraband Western watch.'

'Ha,' says *The-hungry-man-on-the-other-side*, 'ha, ha.' But I sense his spirit isn't really in it.

15

The Palace of Miracles

I knew I hadn't been abandoned. I knew that someone would come in time. But it took two more days. Before I hear the tramp of footsteps outside, the rattle of keys in the lock and then the screech of the hinges, and scrape of the metal door frame on the concrete floor.

A wedge of light beams through the chink. Then Comrade Bruhah himself appears, floodlit, as if onstage, casting a shadow twice the length of his body.

He closes the door behind him and enters into the shade of the cell. He turns the lock and pockets the bunch of keys.

He carries a squarish leather case, like a doctor's valise. And in the other hand he has a metal and canvas folding chair, the kind you'd take on a picnic or to go fishing.

'How are you, Yuri? I was told I'd find you here.'

'Hungry,' I say. 'Do you have any food?'

'Yes,' he nods his concern, 'I suppose you must be hungry. And thirsty too?'

'Thirsty, too,' I agree, all hopeful. 'Have you anything for me to drink right now?'

It is probably true. That urine is better than nothing. But you'd prefer not to face the choice. For me, pee remains a taste to be learned. The first sip always makes me gag.

'You'll have met Comrade Yerkotka?' Bruhah jerks his head in the direction of the dead man, now resting on his side, beneath the mound of straw. 'You'll have had time to get to know each other?'

I shake my head.

'He is uncooperative. He wouldn't answer my questions. And, I daresay, he won't answer to you. But we've grown used to having him around. We've left him here as a reminder, to others passing through. His silence reminds us all — 'It's good to talk'.

'We are living in dramatic, changing times, Yuri. Tragic times. Sorrowful times. The Iron-Man died next Monday . . . '

'Next Monday?'

'Or the day after. Or, perhaps, the day after that.'

'Died of what?'

'Rust. The Iron-Man suffered a fatal attack of rust. A lethal case of oxidation . . . Within the week, it will be announced on the radio. The nation will be shocked. The people will mourn. It is a terrible loss to the Motherland.

We will howl. We will wail. We will struggle to contain our grief.'

'He died last week. Surely?'

'No, he died next week, naturally. Like the Great Leader he was, he thought of everything. Even at the very end. He will choose the most opportune time to die. He will first give us the time to choose his successors.'

'Vislov?' I guess.

'No,' Bruhah frowns. 'Why on earth would it be Vislov?'

I shrug. My big mouth. Open, again.

'Tomorrow I will be elected First Deputy Premier. Malarkov will be Premier. It will come as a complete surprise and a privilege to be chosen to lead the people. I am over-joyed to have won their confidence.'

'Congratulations. You're the Boss now,' I say. 'Can I have some food and water?'

'So, I would have come to see you before, Yuri. But I am busy with affairs of State. Now, I come to tell you that you disappoint me . . . '

'I do?'

'You spend time with the Boss. He confides in you. I give you my protection. You promise to tell me what he says. And what news do you bring me?'

'Nothing?'

'Nothing,' he confirms.

'Can I have some water?'

'In good time ... ' He gestures his impatience. 'You will get what I care to give you. Whatever you deserve. But first tell me what you have to tell me ... '

'I know nothing.'

'Tell me *that* thing ... ' he says. 'That *one* thing ... '

'What thing?'

'You know,' he coaxes, 'that thing that the Boss doesn't want me to know.'

'Oh, that,' I sigh, 'that is nothing, really ... '

That, like a salamander, Bruhah eats his own young. So the Boss says.

But he's caught me out. So I feel obliged. To cough up a few things that the Boss tells me. That he says Bruhah is the Mingrelian Conspirator. That no woman is safe in his company. That maybe he is a cannibal, who eats his victims.

'Can I be honest, sir?'

'I'd like that, Yuri.'

'No offence meant, sir, I'm sure. But the Boss remarked you're a necessary evil. That every good cause finds a use for the devil. He says that Motolov is his right hand, and Myokan is his left hand, and Klimov is his heart, but Bruhah is his arsehole.'

'Yes?' Bruhah arches his brows and nods. 'You see, Yuri. You do know many true and interesting things after all. And I think you know even more than you tell me.'

Bruhah reaches for his case. The lock springs open with a firm metal clack. He takes out a pair of transparent plastic galoshes and pulls them over his polished leather shoes.

'Spills,' he explains. 'Squirts. Spurts. Gushes. These shoes are Nubuck Oxford Loafers from Lazarus Brothers of New York City.'

Then he reaches into the case again and draws out a folded piece of maroon rubber, which turns out to be a butcher's apron, which ties with drawstrings at the waist, and around the neck, covering him from chest to knee.

He's preparing for something or other. Something messy, by the looks of it. But, for the life of me, I can't see what.

'Because it is an expensive suit,' he explains. 'Pure Rayon. Single-breasted. Four buttons. Hugo Boss. First they made uniforms for the Third Reich, now they also make suits for Socialist gentlemen. Under-stated. Same fine quality material. Same crisp cut. Same superior style.'

He swings the case around so now I catch

sight of the array of objects inside. There's a set of carpentry tools — saw, hammer, gimlet, screwdriver, shears and such — and some matt metal implements with sharp edges that look as if they were borrowed from a surgeon. And maybe a dentist loaned a little, some plier-like things for pulling out other things, to complete the collection. It is a neat array. Every last piece has its place, its pocket, or its tray.

Bruhah opens up the folding chair and pats the striped canvas seat.

'Yuri,' he says, 'help me out. I need you to sit here, not slump on the floor like a stringless puppet.'

His politeness is compelling. I oblige him. I sit myself down in his chair. I am relying on him to give me some food. If only I behave.

'Arms on the rests,' he commands. Then he reaches for a roll of tape, which he wraps around, tying my forearms to the metal frame. After that, he tapes round my shins to attach me to the chair legs.

'Welcome,' he says, 'to Hell. We call this place *the Palace of Miracles*.'

'You do?'

'Because people remember miraculous things, here. Out of nowhere. Often, they remember things they never, ever knew . . . '

'Really?'

'I tell you a true story, a for-instance, Yuri. Once, the Boss finds he's lost his favourite briar-wood pipe, taken from his office. He tells me to track down and punish the thief.

'Guess what. Two hours later he finds his pipe. It was in his greatcoat all along. Lit. Burning a hole in the pocket. All's well. So I never have to tell him. That the stenographer and the mail-clerk have already been to the Palace of Miracles, confessed to their crime, screamed to be spared, whimpered to be let out of their misery, and then passed on . . . '

Now, in his apron, with his galoshes on his feet, clutching a small claw-hammer, with his eyes bulging, Bruhah looks like some eager handyman, come to fix some faulty appliance.

'We have been looking for a letter,' says Bruhah. 'We know Comrade Iron-Man wrote it, but we can't find it.'

'A letter?'

'A last letter from the Boss. To those he leaves behind.'

'Yes?' I say.

He stoops and bends his knees. He circles me with shuffling feet, peering at me closely, as if looking for the exact place to start, the way you'd take a tin-opener to a can of herrings in tomato sauce.

'Do you know what I'm talking about?'

'No.'

'Do you know what I'm going to do?'

I shake my head.

'I am going fishing. Like we do in Georgia. Do you know how it works?'

'No.'

'It is not like normal fishing, which is a battle of wits between man and fish. We call it *progressive fishing*. We throw dynamite into the pond. There is a bang and a whoosh and a fountain of water. Then all the fish float to the surface. Many are gutted and cooked already.'

'Yes?' I say.

'So, I will go fishing in your pond, Yuri, and see what fishy stuff comes to the surface. But for this I need force . . . I could tap your little head with this little hammer, until every last bone in your skull is broken. Do you know how that feels?'

'Hurtful?' I guess. 'Horrible?'

'Or I could snip off your fingers with these . . .' He pulls out the shears. He pokes them under my nose. 'Do you know what that means?'

I shake my sorry head. I have seen the tool before. These are shears for cutting metal sheets. The sharp edges are scalloped, like a serrated knife.

'It gives us a schedule, a route map. It affords us both plenty of time. It means you have ten good chances, Yuri. To give me the right, helpful answers. Before I finish your fingers and start on your toes. And do you know why I have chosen your fingers first?'

'No.'

'The hands are very sensitive, the fingers especially, Yuri. So, if I want to touch upon your nerves, this is a good place to go. So you will become a confidential friend of pain. It will tell you all its secrets,' says Bruhah, 'and then you, in turn, will tell me what I want to know.'

Now is the time to confess. To avoid unpleasantness. To prevent inconvenience. And not before time. It's best all round.

'Forgive the childish opinion of a brain-damaged simpleton . . . ' I volunteer. 'No disrespect intended. I'm sorry. But I am a special case. Truly I am. On account of my nerves and the state of my brain. I have a neurological condition. My nerves are wired together strangely, differently to other people. Due to damage. When a tram ran over my head and squashed my brain. Now, fear doesn't work on me. Not the normal way. And nor does pain . . . '

'No. Pain works on everyone,' says Bruhah, 'you cannot excuse yourself from pain. She is a hard mistress. She lets no one duck her lessons.'

'It's this way,' I say. I need to convince him.

'I'm a case-study. Well known. I have been written about. I am 'Boy Z' in *The Handbook of Advanced Traumatic Neurology*, by Doctor Luria. Students answer exam questions about me. I am a sick boy with a damaged mind . . . My Temporal Lobes got scrambled . . . Like a breakfast egg,' I say, 'when something hard and fast ran over my head. Now, whenever anyone tries to hurt me, my left hemisphere throws a fit. All the bullies at school have taken turns to hurt me. But they never get past page one . . . '

It's true. Any strong stimulus starts it off. But especially pain. There's scar tissue in the left-hand side of my brain. It causes the electrical impulses to amplify. That makes them amplify more.

They call it a feedback loop. They call it white noise. Then it passes into the other side of the brain. Then it's like an electrical storm. And, then, all hell breaks loose, all through this boy's mind.

It's then I feel it coming. There's a nauseous swirl. There's the stench of rotting fish and pulses of burning orange light. It feels like my head's being hammered from the inside with a wooden mallet.

So, now I'm going to have a *grand mal*, an epileptic episode. And I fear it's a whopper coming.

I look away from Bruhah who is moving the mouth of his shears around my finger.

The last thing I remember is an unpleasant crunching, splitting sound, as bone yields to steel. Then white hot molten metal pours through my finger into my arm, up through my neck, into my skull. It is flashing light then dark with brilliant blue lightning bolts . . .

And, as I fade out, I hear the peevish complaint of Comrade Bruhah, his voice receding, as if he's speaking from far, far away.

'How can I hurt you properly, you shitty little runt, if you keep throwing a fit whenever I touch you?'

⋆　⋆　⋆

I haven't fallen out of friendship with the tapper on the citizen's telephone, on the other side of the wall. But, our initial delight at talking has waned. Day by day we seem to have less to say to each other. And what we have to say does not seem to quench our souls, or raise our spirits.

To my shame, I am close to ignoring him sometimes. For I often feel sadder and worse, for talking to him.

He tells me he feels weaker, that he needs

216

more water, to keep himself hydrated. No one has visited him now for days. He thinks they have left him to rot. The bastards.

He says he needs more nutrition and liquid than you can readily extract from insects and the odd rodent that passes your way.

Drinking your own water only gets you so far. After a while, you can feel more thirsty, not less.

★   ★   ★

I am running out of jokes to tell him and, anyway, they are poor compensation for a man in his sorry, neglected condition.

'If I die here,' he says, 'take a message to my family, if you survive.'

'Sure, Comrade,' I say. 'But let's make each other a promise. We'll make sure we both survive.'

'Take a message to my son. Tell him I love him. Tell him to keep to his studies. And tell him to choose his words carefully, and try not to speak out of turn . . . '

'I will. Most certainly.'

'His name is Yuri . . . '

'Now, there's a coincidence,' I say, 'because my own name is Yuri. And that's the kind of sensible, school-teacher-advice my father would give me too . . . '

'Then, where do you live?' he asks.

'In the staff block,' I say, 'in The Kapital Zoo.'

'Yuri?' he answers. 'Yuri?'

'Papa,' I sob, 'Papa, Papa . . . Is that truly you?'

'My boy . . . Oh, my boy . . . '

★   ★   ★

Talk? We can't stop. We talk over each other. We talk through each other. We shout. We yell. We laugh. We howl. We chatter through the night. We have so much to say, so much to catch up.

Late on, tired and drained, we get awkward pauses. He gets sentimental. He says a man dies two deaths. Once when his heart stops. And, a second time, when people stop talking about him or remembering his life and character.

He says he always tried to be a good father, but that he could not be a good mother too. He says I must try to forgive him for that.

He says if we are parted now, and don't see each other again, I must do as he said, and not as he did. I must live to help other people, and try to make the world a finer place, and to remember to have children myself. And, if I can lend a helping hand to

218

those in need — people, elephants, or whoever — that would be a fine thing too.

He says when I get home I must look on his bookshelves for Trofim Lysenko's *The Science of Biology Today*. He says I will find certain papers inside, near the centre pages, where no one would be tempted to look, in an otherwise dry, unexceptional book.

We talk football, a holiday we took in Odessa, and the music of Shostakovich, pork chops, chocolate cake, and meatballs in cream sauce, and the character of Fox Terriers. Till, at last, he says he is tired. He must sleep.

SLEEPWELLPAPA

I say.

And he replies —

SLEEPWELLYURIANDLIVEAGOOD-LIFEMYBEAUTIFULBOY

But the next morning there is no answer, so I know they must have come in the night. They must have moved him on.

Poor Papa. I hope they treat him better in the new place. I hope it is better there. Wherever they have taken him. And I hope they feed him well. At last.

I don't really believe in God. But, even so. This world is very odd. As you see with electrons and magnetism. Unlikely things happen. You can never be sure. So, I say a prayer for Papa. Just in case.

At least I got to speak to him and hear that he was well.

16

My Soul for a Hershey Bar

No one comes to my cell. No one answers my taps on the piping. I watch the world go from gloomy grey to inky black, and back again. I am two more days without word or company or sustenance.

I would not be pleased to see Comrade Bruhah again. But for one special, particular detail. Walking behind him there's a guard. And he's bearing a tray of food, and a jug of water. He places it on the ground before me. And I am not slow to fall on it and help myself. Without invitation.

I cannot speak too well of this water.

It is fresh, clear, cold, completely wet, water. So far as I can taste, it hasn't passed through anyone else before. Not once. It hasn't dripped through a crack in the wall. It hasn't been crushed, drop by drop, from a beetle, or squeezed out in a paste from the back end of a dead, matted-haired mouse.

'Yuri, Yuri, my young friend . . . ' Bruhah watches me gulp it down, straight from the jug. He awards me a brilliant smile and a flash of china teeth. He reaches out to hug me, then promptly steps back, sniffing, dabbing a cologne-scented handkerchief to his face. 'How have you been keeping, young man?'

'Not so well,' I croak. Even with the unexpected drink, my throat is sore — dry as sand, crackly as autumn leaves underfoot.

I maybe sound resentful. As far as I'm concerned, he's treated me badly.

'The last time we spoke, I was harsh,' Bruhah concedes. 'Now I have taken advice from Comrade Krushka. He says you are a good boy. Just stupid.

'He says you will help us if only we treat you kindly. He says I need to learn new tricks. He tells me I must learn to play better with other children. He says sugar traps more ants than vinegar. He says I mustn't force entry in everybody I talk to, or break them apart . . . '

'You cut off my finger,' I remind him. 'It's hurt ever since. Look. The stump's got infected. And you left me without a blanket, food or water.'

'Yuri,' he wags a warning finger — he has a complete set, himself — 'it does not pay to bear a grudge.' He arches his eyebrows. He shakes his head. 'In politics, you must learn to be flexible. We must let bygones be bygones. You must forgive and forget, as I do. And then move on. This is the dialectical method. Thesis. Antithesis. Synthesis. Supper . . . '

He tells me that although he taxed me of just one small finger, he left me all the others, attached and entire. He says that, everything considered, in the circumstances, in his experience of these matters, nine fingers and thumbs is a high number to hang onto. Many people end up with far fewer. Especially in the Palace of Miracles. And, anyway, Nature's design gave us spares.

'Would you like a *Hershey Bar*?' he asks.

'What?'

'Favourite Amerikan chocolate bar.' He produces a silver and brown wrapped bar. '*Hershey's are first in favor and flavor*. Five-cent candy bar. You are a lucky boy, Yuri. There are only twenty-three Hershey Bars left in the whole Socialist Union, until the next consignment.'

I do not say it is the best thing I have eaten. Ever. In my whole life. But it comes close to roast goose with crunchy roasted potatoes and spiced red cabbage.

Then I set about the food on the tray.

There's a slice of rye bread, two smallish cold potatoes, half a raw onion, a couple of rounds of raw turnip, a bowl of gruel and two slices of sausage. It takes whole minutes to gobble them all, and then lick the residual smears off my remaining fingers — for the chewing slows me down, and my mouth is still dry.

'There . . . ' Bruhah beams, 'I think we are friends again, aren't we? Now, I want you to do some things for me. What do you say? Are you willing?'

I nod. It is a terrible state of affairs. How your stomach can lead your morals astray.

'We got off to a bad start,' he concedes. 'Let's start over again. You are a lucky boy, Yuri. You are a utensil whose use has come. Like a wooden spoon for stirring the porridge. So, I do not want to hurt you. I want us to be friends.'

'I'll happily do things for you,' I declare, 'but could you do something for me?'

'What do you want?'

'I would like my mother and father back,' I tell him. 'Just that. No more. No less. Mama is in a camp in Kolyma. Papa was here, next door, in a cell.'

'Is that all?' Bruhah smiles. 'Of course. It is yours. I will arrange for you to go where your father has gone. Only it may take a couple of days to arrange.'

Then Bruhah tells me what he wants from me.

He says I spent more time with the Boss than anyone else at the end. He says I must make a list of everyone the Boss saw in his last days. He says I must write down whatever he said. I must remember any phone calls he made, any letters he wrote. He says history deserves to know.

He says that Matryona knows of a letter that the Boss had written. She thinks I must have seen it. It is very important. Do I know of this letter? Where is it?

I tap my head with my knuckles. There's an empty, wooden sound. 'Can you hear?' I ask. 'That's traumatic brain damage,' I explain. 'It can make me foolish. There's scar tissue in the left side of my brain. It causes me to have fits. When I've had a fit, I completely forget what happened before . . . '

'Do you remember a letter?'

I crease my eyes in concentration. I crumple my brow. I bite on my lower lip. I show how hard I am thinking. I am thinking so hard, I'm on the threshold of tears.

I am doing my best. But, as they well know, I'm a stupid child.

'There's something . . . ' I admit, 'at the back of my mind. I believe I saw it once. But — for the moment — I can't remember where it is now.'

'Yes?'

'Do the words *last testament* mean anything?'

'Yes,' Bruhah nods rapidly, with enthusiasm, like a woodpecker. 'They do.'

'Could the letter be written to someone whose name began with an S?'

'Yes,' he agrees. 'Think clearly. Was it Saitov? Samokhin? Surikov? Or Siyan? Sergeyev?'

'Yes,' I agree, 'one of those. Unless the name began with an R.'

'An R?'

'Could be,' I agree.

'Like Reshetnikov? Rodin? Rusnak? Rykov? Ramazanov? Raitov? Ramokhin?'

'Exactly,' I agree, 'Though maybe it began with a T.'

'A T?'

'Don't worry . . . ' I say. 'Give me time. Let me look. Then let me look again.' I tap my empty cranium. 'It will come to me. Out of nowhere. That's how this mind of mine works. I'll be doing something else. Then I'll suddenly remember this letter. And just where I saw it last . . . '

Maybe I can see it now. In the kinema of my mind. But it doesn't pay to be too hasty.

★   ★   ★

Much has changed in a hurry.

The dacha has been ransacked, and

226

emptied of people, possessions and papers. Most of the guards have been sent to other postings, far North or far East, far away from The Kapital.

Matryona is packing. She has been given travel documents, ordered to visit her sister in Yekaterinburg, and stay far away until further notice.

The staff are gone, leaving only a handful of guards. The kitchen has been closed. The library is cleared of books. It has even been emptied of bookshelves. The walls are cleared of pictures. The garage is empty of limousines.

Now footsteps are boomy and echoey on the parquet flooring.

The Iron-Man's study is a bare space. Clean, clear patches on the walls show where the maps and pictures had hung. The desk, bookshelves and filing cabinets have all been taken. Only his armchair, and scuff marks on the parquet flooring, show where the furniture stood before.

★　★　★

It is part of my arrangement with Bruhah that I keep the constant company of Isakov.

Isakov goes with me everywhere. And will stay with me, until I have written down all the

Boss's movements, meetings and comments, and until I find the letter.

I wash with him standing beside me at the basin. I go to the toilet with him by my side in the cubicle. We walk together, hands grazing, close as lovers in Gorky Park. We sleep like spoons in the same iron-framed cot, his chest stuck to my back, an arm wrapped around me.

After a day, we are friends. He softens and grows confidential.

'This is my big chance,' he says.

'Yes?'

'Everyone gets a big chance. Once at least in life. And when it comes, you must seize it with both hands.'

'I guess so . . . '

'Marshal Bruhah has taken me under his wing. He has made me his assistant . . . '

'Congratulations, Comrade,' I say.

'He asked me to do a big thing. A very serious thing. And I did it. It is a thing that makes me a big man. Bigger than you can ever imagine . . . '

'Yes?'

'I cannot tell you what it is.'

'Good,' I say, 'I'd prefer not to know.'

'It is a thing that makes me a figure in history. A thing that can never be undone.'

'Really?'

'The Marshal always looks after his own.'

'Good for him,' I say. 'Good for you.'

'Besides . . . ' Isakov taps his head, 'I know things. I've seen things . . . '

'That will help,' I agree.

But, for my part, I see it differently.

I do not trust Marshal Bruhah. Not with my nose. Not with my fingers. Not with my father's dentures. Not with my family. Not with our future. Not with the Boss. Not with the Motherland.

I reckon I cannot afford to give him all he wants of me, because then he won't need me any more.

So, I calculate I must not recover *That Letter*, with the crabby green writing on the yellow envelope. Even after I find it, where I'd seen it, in my mind's eye, slipped down a crack in the floorboard, under my bed, in the staff dormitory, with a corner rising out, proud of the floor, which needs pushing back in, before Isakov can spot that I've finally found it.

So, we have to spend yet another day looking. Everywhere I have been round the dacha. Upstairs. Downstairs. Inside. And out.

No luck.

Still, we don't give up. It's just a matter of patience.

★   ★   ★

You know something is up. You hear it on the Home Service of Kapital Radio. The nine o'clock morning news is a repeat of the midnight news. The physical exercise broadcast is cancelled. So is the Party Lecture. Instead, they are playing slow, sad music, but not saying why this is a solemn time.

At five minutes to three in the afternoon, the music stops. There is the pealing of bells. Then the National Anthem. Then the voice of Yuri Levikov. Slowly, gravelly, miserably, with a voice cracking with emotion, he announces —

The Central Committee of the Communist Party, the Council of Ministers and the Presidium of the Supreme Union announce with deep grief to the Party and all workers that on March 5th at 9.50 p.m., Josef Petrovich Iron-Man, Secretary of the Central Committee of the Communist Party and Chairman of the Council of Ministers, died after a serious illness.

'The heart of the Great Genius, Kind Uncle, Father of the Nation, and follower of the genius of Lenin's work, the Wise Leader and Teacher of the Communist Party and of the Socialist people, stopped beating.'

'Shit,' says Isakov. 'They took their time to announce that . . . The foreign broadcasts put it out three days ago.'

* * *

Two days later, Bruhah is driven back here to the dacha from The Kapital in his new silver ZIS-110. It flies a red pennant on the bonnet. His chauffeur polishes the bodywork as Bruhah takes Isakov for a walk in the woods.

I watch them trudge between the tall swaying birches. Bruhah has his arm over Isakov's shoulder, his mouth close to his ear. Isakov's head bobs in agreement with whatever is said. It is a fine thing to see the natural friendship between like-minded people overcome all else, even in difficult times.

Then they are swallowed up by the shade of the wood.

There is some huntsman nearby, or a woodsman culling the vermin, because I soon hear the crack of two gun shots, then the angry, answering squawks of some crows.

Bruhah comes out alone, ten minutes later, walking fast with a jaunty step in his muddy boots, wiping his hands with his cravat. He whistles for the driver to start up the car.

For his part, Isakov stays on in the woods.

An hour later. I cross Bruhah's path again. He is striding down the main corridor with the hefty Bulgirov at his side, the long and the short of it — the man who never rests and the man who sleeps in the lavatory. Both regard me as I come level. From Bulgirov I win a delicate wink, a tick of emotion crossing his fat, flat, moon face. From Bruhah comes a cold stare, as if I have awoken an unpleasant idea in his mind.

'Come, Yuri,' says Bruhah, 'we have unfinished business, you and I.'

'No,' says Bulgirov, 'I don't think so.'

'No?' says Bruhah. He swings round, turning his stare on Bulgirov. 'It is my business. It doesn't concern you.'

They are eyeing each other, unblinking, like two dogs facing off, over a bone.

'Our business is complete here,' says Bulgirov. 'We have finished tidying. Our housekeeping is done. Enough is enough.'

'Yes?' says Bruhah. 'Let me decide.'

'Angel-face, here, is my friend,' says Bulgirov, laying his heavy hand on my shoulder. 'He's harmless. He's an idiot. He's a child. He makes me laugh. I wouldn't want to hear he's disappeared, or come to any harm.'

Bruhah clucks and strides straight past me without a further word. I don't think I figure in his thought any more. He must have a lot on his mind, and bigger fish to fry. Or perhaps, I'm just punctuation, a comma in his book and it doesn't really matter if I'm here, or there, or nowhere at all.

I'd wanted to remind him. About his promise to return my parents. But I'm nudged by caution too. I've had enough of his close attention. I can do without any more.

'Do you have a home?' Bulgirov pinches my cheek.

'Yes, sir.'

'Best go there,' he says. 'Best go soon as you can.' And he pats me between my shoulder blades, then turns on his heels without a backward look.

I wander down the corridor to the entrance hall.

Tomsky has been left on his own to guard the front door. He looks up from his book, he leans back in his creaking chair.

'Yuri . . . ' he says, 'you still here, kid?'

I shrug. I realise everything has changed. For the first time since I'd come to the house, there is no task for me, no one holding my collar, telling me what to do.

No one cares about me, here. Not any more. Papa, Bruhah, the Iron-Man, Krushka,

Isakov have other concerns. They had all moved on, each in their own direction. And so must I.

* * *

I collect my possessions from the dormitory. There are two books I'd borrowed from the Boss's library. Soap and a towel I took from the bathroom, together with a plug for a basin. There are some of the Iron-Man's patched-up old shirts that Matryona had handed down to me. And the letter to Vislov from the Iron-Man I recovered from under the bed. Together with the Tokarev TT-33 pistol, and a clip of ammunition, that I found in the guard room, which I kept as a souvenir of my brief holiday, helping out, here in history.

They all go into a small camouflage-pattern parachute-regiment rucksack.

Then I am back on my way to The Kapital, bouncing along the rutted road in the passenger seat of a furniture lorry that stopped to give me a lift.

There are all sorts of excited ideas leaping through my mind.

I wonder if Bruhah had kept his word already, and returned my parents. I'll consider the possibilities when I get home.

Who would be there, bounding forward to hug me, to wrap me in their arms?

Would it be Mama? Papa? Or both together?

17

Return

The signs aren't encouraging. There's no answer to my knock. The spare key is dusty on the lintel. The door swings open on a dark corridor. There is a smell of must and neglect. The air is colder inside than out on the stairwell.

'Mama and Papa,' I call. 'It's me, Yuri.'

There is only silence. Outside the gibbons have quietened their chatter, listening to my call.

'Papa?' I shout. 'Mama?'

I walk through to the kitchen. Our abandoned dinner plates are there on the table. The uneaten noodles have a carpet of furry, blue-green mould. The tea mugs float an oily, surface scum. A scent of rotting onion taints the air.

Papa's newspaper, folded open to the puzzles and chess page, is now weeks old.

I lie on my bed. And cry. Slow, cool and damp first. Then, hot, fast and howling, head-splittingly loud.

There's something comforting in letting it

out. After an hour of that, I have a splitting headache but, in most other respects, I feel much better.

* * *

Later that evening, Papa's friend Comrade Anna, Curator of Elephants, comes calling.

'Roman, Roman . . . ' She hammers her fists on the door.

'It's me, Anna.'

I open up sniffling.

'Yuri. Oh, Yuri . . . ' she says, 'I saw the light in the window. But it's only you . . . ' She wrinkles her face. She was hoping for better.

She wraps an arm around me. She pecks me on the forehead. She is a mixed bag of scents. I detect hay, elephants, warm breath and lemon soap.

'Yuri . . . ' She puts a palm on each cheek and gazes into my face. 'What have they done to your nose?'

'That's nothing,' I say. 'Look at my finger. It isn't there.'

She clucks. She frowns. She shakes her sad head.

She clears the kitchen table. She boils water for tea. We sit. I tell the story. Now and then she reaches out across the tabletop and squeezes my hand.

I can tell from her frowns, wrinkled forehead and raised brows, she's finding it hard to believe all I say. At some points in the tale she asks for detail, or she demands I make things clear. She is concerned I've got the names and people right. And she checks the order in which things happened.

'It was Comrade Iron-Man?' she demands. 'Are you really sure?'

'Yes. Yes,' I say. 'It was Josef — Uncle Joe — all right. He smokes too much. He forgets people's names. He cheats at draughts. He swears like a sentry.'

'You're certain it was him?'

I say, 'Yes, he wanted to shoot all the doctors. And treat everyone like flies. And put an end to love. But there were the three doubles too, of course — Felix, Rashid and Director Dikoy.'

'You sat in his study, you say?'

'Yes,' I say, 'but there were four identical rooms. He used them in turn.'

'And Krushka? You're sure? He was really there?'

'Yes. He can dance the Kalinka,' I explain, 'like a ballerina. But he gets very drunk. Then he sings rude songs about naked ladies.'

I tell her about how I got myself into trouble. Nose and finger.

'Marshal Bruhah?' she frowns. 'How can you be certain?'

But, most of all, she wants to know about Papa's movements, and is less concerned with mine. She is worried to hear of his time in the cell.

'All this is dangerous talk,' she says. 'It may be true. Or, you may be mistaken. No good comes of speaking of it. Take care. Don't mention it any more to anyone . . . Let's pray — pray hard — for your father's safety . . . '

★ ★ ★

The Kapital takes to the streets over the death of Comrade Iron-Man. His body lies in state for five days, in an open casket amongst the marbled columns in the foyer of the Palace of the People.

Crowds gather in Victory Square to hear the speeches from Motolov, Krushka, Bulgirov, Myokan, Bruhah and Malarkov, who bore the red coffin on their shoulders. Over and over, the band play an arrangement of Chopin's funeral march.

At the North End, the Square is blocked by troops, and sheer walls, while the crowds keep flooding in from the South, pushing those in front of them. There is a stampede. It's said thousands are crushed or trampled underfoot, and leave this world with the Great Father.

They say the queue is five kilometres long to wander past and catch a glimpse of the great man in his coffin. I go with Aunt Natascha, Uncle Ivan and cousin Grigory. We join the column, ten people wide, at Patriot Ponds. It takes us seven hours to reach the mausoleum and then another two hours to pass the open coffin.

You catch a brief look at Comrade Iron-Man from a distance of ten metres, as you climb the marble stairs and look across at the red coffin raised on the podium. You can't stop because of the crush of the people behind.

But I never guessed it would upset me so much. To see the body. Just in passing.

Then I start sobbing, without the power to stop.

Aunt Natascha hugs me with pride and addresses the surrounding mourners. 'This boy is a patriot who loved the Great Father, the Genius, Josef Iron-Man,' she announces.

But, in truth, it wasn't that.

No. It was the sight of my dear friend and protector, poor Rashid, lying there. He'd been so kind to me. Now his lips were sealed forever beneath his bushy moustache, with his thick backcombed hair, fleshy ears and the pock marks burned in his cheeks with sulphuric acid, so stiff and cold, and quite lost to me.

And we never got to say farewell.

It was as if the Comrade Leader could never fall ill, or die, without some friend of mine having to match the cost — and suffer the same fate, alongside in sympathy. First Felix. Now Rashid.

I guessed their reasons. The real Comrade Iron-Man must have looked a weary, decrepit, old corpse. They must have wanted a younger, more vigorous, better-looking stiff to put on public display, who presented a more favourable image, sporting a more handsome, energetic rigor mortis.

Besides they are ruthless, I know. And once the Great Leader goes himself, the doubles are dispensable.

★ ★ ★

Comrade Anna says we must regularise our positions — Papa and I.

Otherwise they will dismiss Papa from his post. For not being there. They will reassign the apartment. For being empty. Then, there will be no home to come back to.

Anna has been busy. She has been thorough. She has made all enquiries. But, still, Papa rings no bells.

It is a mystery. But like so many others, he is a man disappeared. Completely and utterly.

The hospitals haven't seen him. No morgue has received him. The Party knows nothing new about him. State Security shows no concern. The Police have no record. His friends have heard nothing.

So Anna arranges through her sister, who is married to Professor Lev Brodsky, Professor of Respiratory Diseases, that Papa obtains a certificate of serious sickness, as a Registered Sufferer of Tuberculosis — requiring three months' recuperation in a Sanatorium in Odessa.

She says people forgive an absence for TB. There's no envy for your holiday. Or your leave on full-pay. They prefer you suffer far away, rather than cough up your sick blood over them.

Still, she says, we must occupy the apartment. Otherwise they will give it short-term to someone else, or they'll bury Papa off before he's coughed his last.

We make a plan of when I go where. The way it works, Comrade Anna comes early morning, and late at night, to check I'm at home and well. And after school, in the afternoon, I go to Aunt Natascha's, eat supper, do my homework, and stay for the evening, before Uncle Ivan walks me home.

Things are always changing here at the zoo. Lotti the giraffe has given birth to a calf called Tippi. She is very sweet-natured, but shy. She lurches about like a drunk on stilts and sometimes topples over.

The Chinese Zoo has sent us a pair of giant pandas, in exchange for a couple of Siberian tigers. Every day hundreds of visitors crowd round in order to witness them hidden in the bushes, or lurking in shadows in the dark of their lair.

Shango, Comrade Elephant, has learned a new trick. He shoots water with his trunk, curled back over his shoulders. He's aiming to hit the Macaque monkeys in the next enclosure, while pretending to look the other way. For their part, they pelt him with rotten fruit. There's no love lost between them.

When Shango hits a monkey, fair and square, he just swishes his tail with pleasure and flaps his ears. But when he knocks one completely off its perch, he raises his head to the heavens and trumpets his triumph.

Like the other Comrade Elephant, he's a character who enjoys his revenge.

★ ★ ★

I still get myself bullied at school.

Sergei Erofeyev has taken to twisting my nose and making the noise of a car horn. Saying, *Honk. Honk. Big Conk.* While Taras Botskin has found some new names, like *Donkey-Sucker, Dick-Up-Your-Arse, Jerk-Off, On-Your-Knees, Drink-My-Spunk, Mother-Licker,* which aim to hurt, but end up contradictory, making no real sense at all. So I've learned to suffer it all in silence.

To be frank, when you've endured the close attentions of Bruhah, their attempts seem conversational, friendly, bordering on kindly.

I don't dare say a word about my adventures. Not even to my new friend Ossip Lokstin. It's dangerous to speak of it and, anyway, I know I won't be believed. So, when our class teacher asks us to write an essay on *What we did on our holiday*, I lie and miss out all the bits about Comrade Iron-Man.

Instead, I say we went to Sparrow Hills and collected wild crowberries.

But at first I get some interest and attention from the rest of the class, on account of my missing finger and bent nose.

I say I lost the finger at the zoo, in an unprovoked attack when I put my hand through the bars of the wolf pen.

18

The Emperor of the Turnstiles

Drunks gather on the triangle of paving, on the benches before the turnstiles to the zoo. They work the visitors for small change and easy pickings. Papa used to say it was one of the purest forms of Socialism. To each according to his thirst. From each according to his heart.

I have to pass between their benches every morning. The gentlemen-of-the-street are sleeping off the bottled pleasures of the night before, or performing their makeshift ablutions at the fountain, surprising themselves once more with water, cascading, all frothy, out of Comrade Gorky's mouth.

Me? I'm off on my way to school.

But this morning, one of the drinkers stands up unsteadily. He starts waving at me, then when I walk on by, he commences yelling. He must think he knows me. He is very determined.

'Idiot boy. Here . . . Come . . . Now . . . I command you.'

I turn his way and trudge up till we are

facing, a metre apart.

He is a short man with a cracked, weather-beaten, liver-spotted, grimy face. His upper front teeth are missing. He is wearing a soiled Army greatcoat. The foil neck of a bottle of Victory vodka sticks out from his side pocket.

He wears a pair of scuffed unlaced infantry boots, above drill trousers that end at his shins. His hair was shaved to the scalp some time before and has grown back to a tufty, uneven crew-cut. He boasts the early, stubbly stages of a silver moustache and beard. The thickest hair on his head is sprouting in tufts from his nostrils and ears.

'Where have you been? I needed you,' he scolds. 'Every day I've been waiting. The tasks have been mounting up . . . '

The gruff voice has a deeply familiar ring. But the man slurs badly. And he has a heavy cold, with mucus dangling like an icicle from his nose. You could see from his shuffling gait, and the collapsed, immobile right side of his face, he had suffered a serious stroke.

There are smells drifting across the divide between us that are sour, acrid, sweet, stale, rotten, fermenting and deeply personal. He smells like the mushy end of the hippo enclosure on a hot summer's day.

'Remind me of your name,' he demands.

'For the moment it escapes me.'

'Yuri,' I say. 'My name is Yuri Romanovich Zipit.'

'Well . . . ' he says, 'idiot child. Surely you recognise *me*?'

'Forgive me . . . ' I shrug. I smile my confusion. Although, in truth, there is something about him that is both disturbing and familiar, knocking in my mind, while ringing the bell, screaming for admittance.

'Here, Lemkov . . . ' The old tramp turns to his neighbour. 'Tell the boy who I really am. Who I *really* really am.'

Lemkov stands up languidly, gives me a heavy wink, clicks his heels together and salutes me.

'I am pleased to introduce his Very Excellency, Emperor of the Turnstiles, High Commander of the Universe, Chairman of the Drinkers' Party, Tsar of Patriarch Ponds, Keeper-of-the-Bottle, and — in his own mind, at least — none other than Josef Petrovich Iron-Man, deceased.'

And then, as I look into the deep, muddied pools of the old man's eyes, I see him at last for who he is. Who he really is.

Yes.

It truly is.

Him. Himself.

The Gardener of Human Happiness.

The Architect of Joy.

The Boss. The Chairman. Kind Uncle. The Genius. The Helmsman. Comrade Iron-Man. But standing before me, strangely diminished in rank and transformed in appearance — from General Secretary of the Communist Party of the Motherland to an unkempt, ripe-smelling, tipsy street-dweller.

'Lemkov was Professor of Psychiatry at The Kapital University,' says the Boss, 'but he got himself sacked for political misjudgements. Now I've had him rehabilitated. He is my Minister for Internal Affairs and Marshal of Everyday Things.' The Boss sniffs, against the tide, to arrest the drippy down-flow of the pendulum of snot. 'And Simionov here is my new Minister for Defence, with Special Responsibility for Scaring off Rascals . . . While Arkadylev is Commissar for Stealing Eats and Begging Small Change.'

'But . . . ?' I gape. I gesture to him, the benches, his companions.

'I look different, perhaps?' The Boss shakes his wearied, weathered head. 'Things are changed. I have been locked out of all my fortresses and palaces. I have no country dacha. I have no town house. No official residence. I live on the streets. I've been shamefully treated. I am waiting for my rescue. To be returned, to where I belong . . . To be put back in charge of the whatsit . . . ' He strains to recall the name for it, whatever it was he governed . . .

'*The Motherland*,' I guess.

'Yes,' he smiles, 'that's the one, and again made top you-know-what, never mind Chairman of the what's-its-name . . . '

'*Politburo*,' I suppose.

'Yes, that's it. Exactly . . . But you wouldn't believe it. I have been denied entry to the Palace of the People. Turned away. The guards spurn me, or lower their rifles, and poke their bayonets my way. The police shout at me and chase us away. I have had to start afresh, to appoint a new Administration, with new Deputies . . . Fyodor, here, replaces Malarkov. I have made him Commander of Bonfires.'

'How has all this happened?' I ask. 'I was sure you were dead. The whole Motherland believes you are dead. People queue to pay homage to your body. It's embalmed, for all to see, in the Palace of the People. There is a new government. Bulgirov is Premier. Bruhah is Deputy.'

'It's Bruhah. The bastard. He did this to me. The evil dwarf . . . '

'How on earth?'

'He comes with armed guards in the thick of night. They break into my room at the dacha. He knows I am planning to have him arrested. He says it is time for me to go — instead of him . . . He says I'm too old and too sick. He says I'm a danger to the Motherland, and a something bad to this, while a threat to something else. But he says he will not have me killed.

' 'There are worse things than death, Josef Petrovich,' he says, 'and I will show them to you. I will condemn you to life. You can see what it is like to live as a citizen in Comrade Iron-Man's Motherland . . . ' '

'Yes?'

'So they pull me out of bed. They tug me into old, ill-fitting clothes. They mess up my appearance. To make me look different. They sit me down and take shears to my head. They clip off my moustache. They pierce me with a nailed block that puts a tattoo on my arm. This gives me a prison number. It shows I was an inmate of a work camp. They put new papers in my pocket. These give me permission to reside in Minsk but not in The Kapital. So they make me an outlaw, even here on the streets. They label me an anti-social element. Guess what my papers call me?'

'What?'

'Tinmann . . . Man-of-tin . . . Nikolai Tinmann. A Roma, a Gypsy, who has served twelve years in the Gulag.'

'And then?'

'They pour vodka down me. And they pour vodka over me. To make me sound drunk and smell like a sop. They give me an injection. They say it is some medicine to help horses relax. They say I will feel better for it. They smear my coat with dirt and garbage.

''There . . . ' they admire, 'now, you are a proper tramp and a true drunk.' Then they laugh. As if they have done something clever.

''Now . . . ' says Bruhah, 'you are a stupid old beggar. You are weak in the head. You can go where you like. You can say what you like. You can pass any edict. You can write any list. You can make all the Five Year Plans your heart desires. You can threaten who you like . . . No one will ever recognise you. No one will ever believe who you are. Now Comrade Iron-Man is dead. At last. And, if there was a God, I would thank him . . . '

'They drive me into The Kapital. They stop the limousine when they pass a group of drunks gathered round a bonfire. Bruhah gets out of the car and summons two of the drinkers — Lemkov, here, and Simionov. He gives them a good talking to. He reaches into his pocket and hands them some paper money. When he returns to the car, he tells me, 'Here you are, you disgusting old drunk.' He pushes me out into the freezing air. 'This is your new palace, and these are your new staff.'

'Then they drive off, leaving me to make the best of it all. I address the tramps. I tell them to gather round. I tell them to stand easy. I give an impromptu speech. I tell them who I am. I tell them what I expect of them. I give a brief summary of our current economic planning. I talk of the strategic needs of our nation. I warn them of the hegemonistic machinations of Amerika. I name her Kapitalistic lackeys. I outline our Short-Term Policies. I stress the need for excellence and diligence, both in Manufacture and Agriculture. I explain I am in charge of many important things, including Countries, Cities, Committees, and Commissions, Colleges, Collectives, Cars, Cooperatives and Councils and such. I ask for their cooperation in restoring me to full power.

'They say, 'Fine, old fellow. No problems. But best wait until morning. Just relax for the night. Take a drink, perhaps.' And comforting words like that.

'They are considerate, helpful and polite. They treat me like an elderly uncle. Lemkov gives me a vegetable crate to sit on, close by the fire. Simionov gives me a hot tea laced with vodka to warm my bones.

'But, before long, two policemen come by.

252

They are different. They are insolent. They are insubordinate. Their badges and police hats have gone to their heads. They kick snow on our bonfire to douse it. They tell us all to move on. They are not good Comrades. They are not polite.

''Come here,' I tell them, 'and do as you are told. You scum. I am Comrade Iron-Man. You must take me immediately to the Palace of the People. And I will forgive your earlier insolence . . . '' He shakes his head.

'And?' I ask.

'You won't believe what they do.'

'Do they mistake you for a drunk?'

'The first policeman says, 'If you are Comrade Iron-Man, I am Catherine the Great, so lick my fanny and kiss my arse.' And the second policeman says, 'Go fuck yourself, you old sack of shit.'

'Then he smashes his rifle butt into my mouth and knocks out my front teeth. The other kicks me from behind in the kidneys while I'm sprawled on the ground. They both call me very bad, insolent names, while stamping on me very hard. If Simionov, here, hadn't come to my rescue, I think they would have finished me off.'

'Shame,' I console. 'Shame on them.'

'I have their names and numbers,' says the Boss. 'I have collected the names of all those who have done me wrong, these last few weeks . . . I have suffered a deal of rudeness, doses of contempt, much neglect and disregard. Some people just pass me by and ignore me entirely. I have made a list of two hundred and sixty-five traitors. Some repeat offenders. When I am back in power, I will line them all up, and have them all shot.'

'Life can be difficult,' I observe. As I know from my own bumpy ride.

'Difficult times. But exciting times. And important times. It's like life before the Revolution. We live like desperados and outcasts. We must keep two steps ahead of the police. We must meet in secret. We must liberate food and money to meet our needs. We must be constantly vigilant for traitors amongst us . . . Do you see the hunched man over there, under the tree?'

'Isn't it Pakulin, a guard from the dacha?'

'Exactly,' says the Boss. 'He was in my personal detachment. He guarded my person. Now he works for Bruhah. He follows me wherever I go. I believe he reports back . . . Some days, Bruhah comes by himself, to see how I am. He laughs at my condition. He insults me to my face. But he wants to keep me alive . . . '

'Are you sure?'

'Yes, because he gives Lemkov and

Simionov vodka and money, to keep me safe. 'Look after the Great Leader,' he says. 'I'm happy if he suffers but keep him this side of the grave. I enjoy watching him out on the streets.''

'At least he looks after you.'

'He wants to humiliate me. He delights in seeing me brought low. He says this — 'Some people enjoy the ballet. Some people love the opera. Some people like watching football. But my secret pleasure, Koba, will be watching you . . . ''

'What will you do?'

He splays his helpless palms. He shakes his bewildered head. 'No one ever recognises me for who I am. That corpse in that coffin gets all the praise and respect — and it's not even mine. I get only abuse and neglect. People take me for a tramp, some drunk . . . '

'Yes?'

'It is hard to get even the most basic comforts of life. The shopkeepers want paying — with *money* — for everything. When I say who I am, they throw me out of the shop. Now, they won't let me back through the door.'

'Can I help?' I ask. It was habit. A reflex kindness. But I regret it as soon as the words leave my mouth. The Boss has never been modest in making demands.

'We must mobilise a counter-force. We must arrange a plenary of the Grand Council of the Party. Then I can show myself. And then I can be restored to power . . .'

He says I must seek out Motolov and Myokan for him. He says I can find them at the Palace of the People. I must tell them what has transpired . . . That Bruhah and Krushka have falsified the death of Comrade Iron-Man. But that Iron-Man is alive and poised to return.

'Go. Go,' he urges. 'Tell them the good news.'

'Oh.'

'And one other thing, Yuri . . .'

'Yes?'

'I need chickens.'

'Chickens?'

'Two spit-roast chickens. A suckling pig. A broiled pike with crayfish tails. Two loaves of freshly baked rye bread. A pat of butter. Tomato salad. Aubergine puree. A bag of walnuts. A jar of assorted pickled mush-rooms. Two kilos of grapes. A litre of fresh crowberries. A crate of Georgian wine . . . I think we all deserve a feast. Do you know how long it is since my Comrades and I ate a good meal?'

'Where would I get all those?'

'From a food shop, idiot boy. Demand

them. Explain they are for Comrade Iron-Man. Say, if they refuse me, I will have them all shot.'

'Boss,' I say, 'Comrade Iron-Man is dead. Everyone knows. And the food you want is not there to be had. It can't be bought. Sometimes a shop has tomatoes. But it won't have chickens. And if it ever did have chickens, by some odd chance, it would not have any butter. These foods do not happen together, in the same place, in the same year, in the same city, except in a recipe book from olden times, or a Westerner's imagination.'

As I turn to go, he makes me promise again. That I will go to Myokan and Motolov and inform them of the situation. So they can timetable the Revolution, and come and rescue him.

I say, 'Yes. Of course, Boss.' But I feel guilty. For it isn't a promise I can carry out. And, in truth, I'm not going to try.

The mighty left open their doors, and let me peek inside their lives. But I know, as they know, I am not one of them.

I am a twelve-year-old boy. People take me for a brain-damaged simpleton. There are limits to what I am free to do. I have to raise my hand in class to go visit the lavatory. When I go to buy bread, the baker ignores me.

I cannot be pleading a petition for a dead General Secretary of the Communist Party, recently deceased, to two senior members of the Politburo, Chief Marshals of the Slavic Union.

It is beyond my station. And I cannot convince them Comrade Iron-Man is still alive when he is lying embalmed, for the world to view, there in the Palace of the People.

But beyond that, I've learned this. There is a time to do something. And a time to do nothing. And, in my heart, I know this — best leave alone. Things are better now, these last few weeks.

I don't like to speak ill of a Comrade, but it is better if the government of the Motherland is not just one angry man. Who has lost his memory. And wants revenge. And treats us like flies.

19

Goodbye, History

I never needed *The Daily Truth* to tell me that Marshal Bruhah was a bad man and a cruel character. I knew it from my own experience, when he broke my nose. And I had it confirmed when he chopped off my finger.

And I knew it from the Boss's account — of how Bruhah had forced him out of his dacha, stole his power, and forced him to live as a tramp on the streets.

Yet, he was the cruel man I had trusted. He had promised me the return of Mama and Papa. It was an agreement we'd struck. And I'd believed him. I'd trusted that he set in motion whatever it took for them to be freed and to find their ways home.

And, in no time, with the Iron-Man gone, things had started loosening up. The Supreme Presidium had declared an amnesty for inmates of the Gulag. Many are to be freed — all those serving less than five years; those convicted of military or economic crimes; any women with children under ten; juveniles up to eighteen; men over fifty-five; women over fifty; anyone with an incurable disease. And if Mama is not precisely amongst these, I knew it would not be long before she could follow on, and find her road home.

Two weeks later, I am on the tram to school when I see the news on the front page of *The Daily Truth*. Bruhah, the high and mighty Bruhah, Deputy Premier, has been arrested.

In the Council of Ministers, Krushka and Malarkov had spoken out against him. Troops suddenly appeared in the chamber, out of the blue, to arrest him.

The paper says he has committed treason. For forty years. He has plotted with foreign nations against the Motherland. He has conspired to end Communism and bring back Kapitalism. He has plotted to disarm the Nation's army. He has planned to seize power.

There is a large photo on the cover of *The Daily Truth*. The caption says: *The Fascist Bruhah hangs his head in shame at his arrest for treason.*

The photo showed it. He did hang his head. He did look ashamed. You don't have to be a lawyer to know that sedition and treason are a bad set of crimes to have on your charge-sheet.

But, whoever he was, he wasn't Bruhah.

Not the real Bruhah. Not the one I knew.

This was a leaner, taller man, with more hair on his scalp, and a narrower face and thinner lips, with steel-rimmed spectacles instead of pince-nez.

It was lazy. They'd photographed someone who looked quite like him. Not a proper double. For there wasn't any really close likeness. So I wondered what had happened to the real Bruhah. And would he still keep his promises to return Mama and Papa?

★　★　★

I used to watch the Boss from a distance, morning and evening, but I hadn't seen him around for several days, not on the benches outside the zoo.

'Excuse me, sir,' I ask of Lemkov, 'but where's the Emperor these days?'

'Ah . . . ' says Lemkov. 'The Emperor . . . ' He looks sorrowfully down to his feet. He shuffles his boots. 'Thereby hangs a tale.'

'Is he not well?'

Lemkov looks away, sucks hard and considers, then spits some phlegm to the side of my feet. 'Regarding the Emperor, there is mixed news, both uplifting and dispiriting, happy and sad . . . '

'Tell me the sad, first.'

'He is gone.' Lemkov nods emphatically. 'There is no getting around it. He is stone-cold, dead, departed, passed over, moved on, deceased, stiff as a stick. Dead as a Mastodon, stony as a fossil. We won't see the likes of him again.'

'Whatever happened?'

'Last week some thugs set on him. Stole his coat and boots. Then pushed him into the lake. It was a freezing night. We saw him go in. We didn't see him come out.'

'Murder? For old boots and a torn coat?'

'He was throwing his weight around. Telling people what to do. Threatening to have them shot. Ordering them off to The Cold Lands, and such, for fifteen years or more. Seizing their possessions for himself. Saying it was State Property. It doesn't go down well. It isn't comradely. It isn't Socialistic. People object. It gets on their nerves . . . It stands to reason. Folk who live on the streets mostly want more vodka. They don't want taxation, and they don't want more government.'

'The good news?' I sniff. Tears are forming against my better judgement, smearing my cheeks, misting my eyes. The Boss was a difficult customer, no doubt. But he'd looked after me, in his harsh way, and made himself my friend.

'The good news,' says Lemkov, 'is that the

crazed, demented old bastard is no longer in pain.'

'Yes,' I say. 'He wasn't happy. Not at the end.'

Lemkov tells me the tale.

'The yellow dwarf used to give us money to look after him. He said he would have us arrested if any harm came to him. But then he stopped coming. There was no more money.' He rubs empty fingers against naked thumb. He looks hopefully at me and down to my pocket.

'I only have thirty-seven kopecks.'

'Every little helps.' His hand closes around the coins and imprisons them in his fist. 'Myself, I didn't mind the old man, even though he acted like he was Tsar of Greater Slavia, and shouted at us, and gave us stupid titles and idiotic jobs to do. Not as long as I was paid to look after him . . .

'In my old capacity as psychiatrist, I would have diagnosed him as a Paranoid Schizo-phrenic. He had delusions of grandeur. He believed he was a great and powerful man. He thought the world was trying to do him down. All this was compounded with vascular dementia and the destructive toll of a series of strokes. Alongside he had Korsakoff's Syndrome — which prevented him remembering anything new, which stopped him learning in life . . .

'But it is hard, here on the streets. It is not a kind place. This is not a Sanatorium. Nor an Asylum. The crazed have to look after themselves, same as the sane, the drunks, the outlaws and addicts.

'We can barely raise a bonfire, and brew a samovar. So we do not have the facilities to run a psychiatric clinic and safe-house for demented old misanthropes who think they rule the world. We listen to each other's problems. We are sympathetic. We help if we can. But we do not offer systematic pharmacology, convulsive therapy, lobotomies or talking-cures . . . '

I patted Lemkov's arm. 'See you, Comrade,' I said. I wished him good-day, and a good life.

★　★　★

But I thought to myself — *Who knows?* You could never be sure with the Boss. He was a tough old bird. It took more than his death, by poisoning, freezing, drowning and strokes, to keep him down. He had more lives than a cat.

Maybe he swam to the other side of the lake, warmed himself up with a bonfire, added another two names to his back-pocket list — 'People to be shot' — then took himself off somewhere else. Gorky Park? Sparrow Hills? The Arch of the Unknown Martyr?

He'd seized power once before. He was older now, if not wiser. He knew how it was done. Maybe he couldn't manage ruling an entire Union of Republics, or a whole country. But he could certainly boss a gang of all-day drinkers in one of our Kapital's parks.

★ ★ ★

Life scribbles on you. Like vandals scrawl on walls. You learn a lot of lessons along the way. Some of them useless. Some of them valuable.

> **Even the greatest of men have their faults.**
> **In times of drought, you can drink your own urine.**
> **Nature gives you spares, so nobody needs every last finger.**
> **But you should take good care of your Papa, he's the only one you get.**
> **Even the biggest things topple in time.**
> **Love is a liberal waster, and has no respect for the Party.**
> **You never know what will happen to a soul — they could get doubled,**

disappeared or disinvented.

It's not the votes that count, it's the man that counts the votes.

Where there's a person, there's a problem.

Always look in the box, before you bury the coffin.

The writer is the engineer of the human soul.

You know how it is with a library book. You didn't take it back. Now it's late. Because it's late, you put off taking it back. Now it's later still, so you delay some more.

It just gets worse. And the worse it gets, the worse it is, still. And you wake up to find you owe three whole roubles.

That's the way it was with the letter. Comrade Iron-Man's last letter. That Marshal Bruhah wanted so much —

The last testament of Josef Petrovich Iron-Man General Secretary of the Central Committee naming his successor

I had it in the tin box of private things that I kept under my bed. I owed its delivery to a Comrade called Vislov.

I asked a teacher at school who knows

266

about politics. And, it turns out, this Comrade Vislov is not unknown.

First name, Mikhail. Patronymic, Andreyevich. He has a seat on the Politburo. He's Chairman of the Commission for Foreign Affairs, which means he gets to say what we do abroad.

Sometimes I look for the easy way out. I was still hoping that the letter didn't really matter.

The envelope wasn't properly sealed, just stuck in the centre. So you could open it with a knife, then glue it all back properly. I am hoping it says something ordinary, unimportant, like —

Thanks for the parcel. See you next Thursday.

or —

Sorry you fell off your bicycle. Hope you get well soon.

Then I wouldn't have to worry about non-delivery, or the terrible delay. But, no. When I open the letter and peek at the first page, it confirms then inflates my very worst fears.

It is very political. It is very personal. Names get named. Blames get blamed. Insults are aimed. Crimes get called. Angers flare. Characters are called into question. Old wounds are opened. Comrade Iron-Man has some very harsh words for his colleagues and friends.

As goodbyes go, it is not a fond one.

I, Josef Petrovich Iron-Man, declare that I have dedicated my life to increasing the Gaiety of the Motherland, labouring unstintingly for the joy and happiness of its peoples.

And yet I have been betrayed, grievously, by the actions of my so-called Comrades, yapping and snarling like a pack of jackals.

Let it be known that Marshal Bruhah is a character of the most depraved, perverse and sadistic character, unfit for leadership or government, and a rapist, murderer, torturer, as any forensic examination of his home will reveal.

Let it be known also that Comrade Nikita Krushka is a barbaric and vicious character responsible for the murder and imprisonment of legions of honest workers in the Borderlands in atrocities conducted behind this General Secretary's back, without his permission or knowledge . . .

It goes on and on. With loads of *insofar-ing* and plenty of *letting-it-be-knowns*. There's seven pages of it. In spidery green writing. He has a bad word to say about everyone — Bulgirov, Malenkov, Motolov, Myokan . . .

He regrets that the gaiety of Slav life has been soured by his barbarous colleagues, doing this and that behind his back, like shooting people, letting them go hungry, or putting them into prison. He concludes by saying that Vislov alone is fit to lead the Party.

★　★　★

It burns a hole in my pocket, this letter. It scorches a guilt in my mind. And the longer I leave it, the worse the burn.

Perhaps, it's best to hand it in to the authorities — a police station, State Security, or the Party office.

I could say, 'I found it on the street.' Then explain, 'Of course, I haven't read it.'

Then, I wouldn't be in any trouble.

★　★　★

It was a hard road with a heavy load. It had worn me down. All this time with top people, helping out in history.

I find the book that Papa had mentioned — Trofim Lysenko's *The Science of Biology Today* — on the top row of shelving behind his desk. It was large and fat — the size of a box briefcase — but strangely light.

He had cut out the centre of the pages with a razor to make a box-like cavity. Within were two brown envelopes.

On one, Papa had written *For emergencies*, in red ink, and had underlined it twice. Inside was a wad of banknotes. Musty-smelling. Colour, green. Currency, US Dollars. Denomination, hundred notes. Total value, three thousand five hundred. Which — if the dollar is worth even half as much as the rouble — is a deal of money.

On the second, fatter, envelope, Papa had written *Valeriya*, my mother's name.

Inside was their wedding photograph. Mama is young with blonde wavy hair and a smile to warm December. Papa, alongside, looks serious, older, plainer and lucky, in a starched collar and striped suit.

With the photo were all her papers and certificates, neatly folded and in order of issue. Birth certificate, school exams, Membership of the Junior Pioneers, Violin aptitude — Grade 7, Gymnastic Awards, Medical Graduation, Gold Medal Prize for Surgery, Order for Outstanding Medical Research, Conviction under

Article 58 for Counter-Revolution, and then her death certificate.

Date: July 1951.
Place: Kolyma Detention Camp.
Status: Serving Prisoner.
Cause of death: Cardiac failure.

I guess Papa hadn't wanted to tell me. He'd thought to protect me.

I had no memories of Mama, only hopes I'd posted forward, to hold for the future. Like a parcel saved up for my name day. So Papa hadn't wanted to deprive me entirely.

★   ★   ★

But it came right out of the blue. Like a sucker punch to the belly.

You double up. You feel winded and dizzy. Your breath won't come. You can't move. Your body just won't obey your brain.

It's a sudden, unexpected way to lose your mother.

I weep, of course. Then my sick mind takes over.

I throw a big fit, thrash around, graze my knees, bruise my head and bite my lip.

Then, next day, I feel much better.

At least, I still have Papa.

And I'll value what I've got.

I've polished his best pair of boots. They're waiting for him beside the front door.

I've put fresh, ironed sheets on his bed. I've laid out clean shirts and underwear in his drawers.

I know what it's like to go without food, and to be starved of all you crave. So, I've started a collection of some of his very favourite things, as treats to welcome him back: a hundred grams of Pushkin's Spiced Pipe Tobacco, a quarter bottle of schnapps flavoured with caraway seed, a jar of peppermint bonbons, an unopened pack of Hero of the Revolution Tea, a quarter kilo of macaroni made from real semolina flour.

It's just a matter of patience. And never letting any dark doubt cloud your horizon. So, I'm just awaiting his return — whenever, from wherever.

Other titles published by Ulverscroft:

FROM THE HEART

Susan Hill

1950s England: Olive is a happy, open-hearted girl, whose (somewhat tricky) mother is dead, and who lives with her father in a solid Edwardian house with apple trees in the garden. Her passion for books gets her easily into university, where the world is surely waiting for her. There, she meets a boy. But then Olive makes a mistake — the kind anyone could make — and faces an impossible choice. Still young, and full of hope, she can't possibly know how that mistake will sit in her heart for the rest of her life . . .

THE WOMAN ON THE STAIRS

Bernhard Schlink

On business in Australia, a widowed German lawyer visits an art gallery. There, he encounters a painting entitled *Woman on Staircase*. He knows this work — and its subject: Irene Gundlach, the woman for whom he once risked everything . . . As a young man, the lawyer became entangled in the affairs of three people mired in a complex and destructive relationship: the woman, her husband, and the artist who depicted her. Now, remembering those long-ago events, he sets out to track down the painting's owner — and the woman on the staircase herself . . .

THE SONG OF THE STORK

Stephan Collishaw

As the Second World War burns through Europe, a fifteen-year-old Jewish girl is on the run in the Polish countryside, having narrowly escaped the German soldiers. Now Yael is alone, with only the memory of her brother Josef — fighting with the Red Army far away — to sustain her. Desperate and determined, she seeks shelter on the farm of the village outcast. Aleksei is mute and solitary, and wary of hiding a Jew. But, as the brutal winter advances, he reluctantly takes her in ... and a delicate relationship begins to flourish between them in their private sanctuary.